Out of the Blue

ESPECIALLY FOR GIRLS™
presents

Out of the Blue

By

Barbara Bartholomew

SIGNET
VISTA

This book is a presentation of
Especially for Girls™
Weekly Reader Books.

This book is a presentation of Especially for Girls™,
Weekly Reader Books. Weekly Reader Books offers book
clubs for children from preschool through high school.
For further information write to: **Weekly Reader Books,**
4343 Equity Drive, Columbus, Ohio 43228.

Especially for Girls™ is a trademark of Weekly Reader
Books.

Published by arrangement
with Signet Vista/New American Library.

PUBLISHER'S NOTE

Cover illustration by Jean Meyer

1

The temptation was too great. Stacy bent over to take off her sneakers and roll up the legs of her jeans. She walked on the cool, wet sand with bare feet, feeling the grit between her toes, then the warm water of the Gulf of Mexico lapped around her feet, submerging them briefly before moving out again. She laughed aloud. Here she was with an afternoon alone at the beach to work out her problems and instead she was wading like a little girl.

The sound of gulls shrieking as they swirled over her head combined with the roar of the surf to drown out her laughter. Her feet and ankles grew chilly in the air and she moved further out to be caught by another white-crested wave as it pounded in. It was her favorite kind of day, cool and misty. Most people stayed away in this kind of weather so that she had the beach largely to herself.

She frowned suddenly at the sight of a van up ahead. Someone had the nerve to intrude on her privacy. Well, she would pretend it wasn't even there and would stroll past as though she didn't notice.

"Hey, there!" It was hard to ignore the shout, but she kept walking.

"I need help," the voice called.

There was nothing to do but turn around. A tall, blond-haired boy wearing jeans and no shirt was leaning around the van to call to her—obviously a tourist. The natives weren't optimistic enough to assume that the fact that this place was billed as a winter paradise meant they could go around only half-dressed on a chilly late February day. Then she happened to spot her own bare toes and wiggled them happily in the sand. Most natives!

She ambled over toward him. "What's the trouble?"

His grin was shy, but there was something likable about it. "I'm stuck."

She should have guessed. Tourists were forever straying off the roads and into the dunes and beaches. "Happens all the time. On days when the beaches are busy, tow trucks make regular runs up and down the beach just rescuing people—for a fee."

"A fee? Guess I don't have much choice. I've tried and tried to get out. Now if I only had a shovel. . . ."

She grinned, her usual, bubbly good humor coming back. After all, it wasn't his fault he'd disturbed her "alone" day. "Sorry, I don't have a single shovel on me."

He looked rueful. "It's the towing service for me then, no matter what it costs."

She glanced thoughtfully at his little van. It was old and battered. Maybe he had been stupid to have gotten stuck, but obviously he didn't have money to throw away.

"Look," she said. "I live over on the mainland, but I do have friends who own a place over here on the island. Maybe we can borrow a shovel from them."

His face brightened. "Great!"

She looked back in the direction from which she'd come. "My car is parked a couple of miles back down the beach. It'd be closer to walk to my friends' house."

"Let's go then." He pulled on a shirt before joining her down on the beach. He stuck out a hand for her to shake. "I'm Ted Lorimer. Down here doing some research."

He seemed young to be on his own. "You and your family," she suggested.

"Nope, all by myself."

It was hard to imagine someone so close to her own age being able to go off on his own. She couldn't help being a little envious. Sometimes she felt surrounded by family.

"You haven't told me your name," he reminded her as they trudged up the beach side by side.

"I'm Stacy Whitman," she said brightly. "I'm 16 and I live in Port Isabel with my grandmother."

"That's the town just across the bay?"

She nodded. "Where do you live, Ted?"

He seemed to hesitate before answering. "Right now, my family is in Chicago."

"Chicago," she repeated, trying to think of something nice to say about a city that was only a name to her. "I hear it's big."

His face looked sad until he smiled. "And Port Isabel is small."

She shrugged. "We like it that way."

"Don't blame you." He sounded close to anger and she wondered what she'd said to make him mad. Well, she wouldn't spend any time worrying about it. She was doing him a favor, not the other way around.

They walked in silence for several minutes. Finally he spoke. "It's really great of you to help a stranger this way."

She smiled, deciding that he wasn't mad at her, but at someone else. Maybe it had something to do with why he was here by himself so far from home.

She couldn't help thinking how different he was from Dwayne. Dwayne would have been talking away and trying to get her to say something. No question but that her steady had a way about him. She grimaced at the thought. Everyone was always telling her how lucky she was to have Dwayne.

She looked uneasily at the boy at her side. Dwayne wouldn't

approve of this. He'd say she should have walked right past the stranded van.

She wished he would say something. It would be easier if they talked. She tried to get the conversation going. "I love the beach. I come over every chance I get."

His smile flooded his gray eyes, making them less cool. "Most people don't know South Texas has such nice beaches. They think you have to go to California or Florida or someplace like that."

She was pleased at the compliment to her region. "I feel like a native," she confessed. "I wasn't born here, but I moved down when I was only two."

"You're lucky," he said again and then didn't say anything else.

He certainly wasn't like Dwayne. Getting him to talk was hard work. And he didn't even seem to expect her to say anything if she didn't feel like it. Dwayne always teased her that she was being boring if she weren't constantly chattering to him. He put a lot of importance on people's being good company.

Suddenly she realized what she was doing. She was comparing Dwayne with this boy she hardly knew. How could she do such a thing?

"We're almost at the Sandersons'," she said, pointing ahead to where a scattered row of beach houses appeared in the distance. "It's the second one down."

As they approached, she was pleased to see a plump, cheerful-looking woman come out from a pretty cottage that rested on what looked like long, wooden legs. Behind the row of houses, the gulf tossed, deep-blue waves frosted with foam. Stacy waved. "Hi, Marti," she called. "We need to borrow a shovel."

"Whatever for? No snow to shovel like back at home."

Stacy grinned. "The Sandersons are from Michigan," she explained to Ted. "They spend winters here."

Before she had a chance to introduce Ted, Marti Sanderson made an embarrassing mistake. "You must be this Dwayne I've been hearing so much about." She beamed at Ted.

Stacy gulped. "No, Marti. This is Ted Lorimer. And the reason we need the shovel is because his van is stuck in the sand."

"Oh, of course." Marti Sanderson dusted her hands energetically to cover her embarrassment. "I'm not sure where my husband keeps the shovel, but if we poke around in the storage shed, most likely we'll find it."

The shed was well-organized but overstocked with an assortment of equipment. "My husband likes to think of himself as do-it-yourselfer. He's always buying some gadget he'll never use."

"I'll find it," Ted said, striding purposefully into the crowded little shed while Stacy and Marti Sanderson waited outside.

Mrs. Sanderson took immediate advantage of his absence. She grabbed Stacy's arm. "He's very good-looking, Stacy, but from what your grandmother said I'd thought you were practically engaged to this Dwayne. She seemed so pleased."

"Not engaged," Stacy whispered back furiously. "We're going steady. I'm only 16, Marti. I don't plan to get married for years and years."

"But your grandmother said. . . ." Marti Sanderson glanced uneasily into the shed, then lowered her voice. "Does Dwayne know about Ted?"

"There's nothing to know! I just met Ted on the beach and offered to help dig out his van."

Ted came out of the shed, shovel in hand. Stacy could only hope he hadn't heard what they were saying.

"Now we can get Ted's van unstuck," she said. "I'll bring the shovel back later."

Marti Sanderson rubbed her hands together. "Oh, dear, I really should drive you back down the beach, but my husband has the car and I just can't say when he'll get back. Perhaps you could come in and have a snack while we're waiting for him."

"Thanks a lot, Mrs. Sanderson, but I want to get back before my van gets ripped off. I live in it and practically everything I own is inside."

Marti Sanderson's eyes grew wide. "You live in a van?"

"Right now I do."

Mrs. Sanderson looked uneasily at Stacy. "Well, some vans are really plush these days."

"Not mine, I'm afraid. Thanks for the loan of the shovel. I'll drop it by once I've gotten the van out." He turned to look at Stacy. "Thanks a lot for helping."

He moved away and she watched him leave with a funny feeling. She'd probably never see him again, but what did it matter?

She didn't even make a conscious decision. "Wait, Ted," she called, running to catch up to him. "I'll help you dig."

He didn't even look particularly pleased. "If that's what you want."

She had to run to keep up with him. Somewhere behind them, she could hear Marti Sanderson's vague protests.

It didn't take long for him to dig sand away from the tires. "Climb in and see if you can drive out," he called.

Stacy hopped into the van. She couldn't help taking a quick look around as she started the engine. It was as neat as Mr. Sanderson's storage building and as full. She saw a bedroll and pillow, an ice chest, and a stack of clothing. Maybe he wasn't kidding and he really did live in this thing.

She started the van and drove easily out of the sand, not stopping until all four tires rested on the firm surface of the road. She got out to wait until he came jogging up.

"Better stick to regular roads from now on," she advised, grinning.

He grinned back, his silvered eyes warm on her.

"That'll be hard, considering I plan to camp on the beach."

"You're going to stay out here at night by yourself?"

"Sure, I already did last night. The camping fee is a whole lot less than the cost of a motel. And it was really great listening to the surf pounding. Once I looked and saw lights way out. Looked like the boats were about to fall off the edge of the world."

"Those were probably shrimpers. Lots of them come into my grandmother's restaurant to eat. They say she's the best cook in town."

"Have you ever been on one of the boats?"

"Sure, lots of times."

He shifted from one foot to the other, looking as if he hated to leave. "How about if I take you back to your car?"

She was suddenly shy, an emotion she rarely experienced. "I can't. My grandmother would have a fit if I went riding around with a stranger."

"We aren't exactly strangers. We both know this nice lady named Mrs. Sanderson."

Stacy laughed. "Still, I'd better not. It won't take me long to walk back."

His expression grew serious. "And Dwayne wouldn't like it?"

Her face heated. She knew it must be red as an apple. How much had he heard?

He put the shovel in the back of the van and climbed behind the wheel. "Don't let them talk you into anything, Stacy. Sixteen is too young to be getting serious about any guy."

He started the engine and, without even saying good-bye, drove slowly off.

She watched him go, feeling unreasonably sorry that it was over. She hoped he would remember to return the Sandersons' shovel.

She glanced at her watch and discovered it was nearly four-thirty. And she'd promised to help during the evening rush!

No way could she make it on time now. She hurried down

the beach without pausing to admire the waves or the dunes. By the time she got back to where she'd parked Grandmother's station wagon, rain was beginning to fall.

Windshield wipers flashed in front of her as she left the island by way of the causeway that connected it to the mainland. After a few minutes, the few lights already lit in the rainy afternoon glimmered through the fog and mist.

Usually Stacy loved rainy weather, but this evening her mood felt as heavy and gray as the weather. She'd gone over to spend her Sunday afternoon on South Padre Island, hoping to figure out what was wrong with her life lately. But she'd hardly had a chance to think things through. Instead she'd ended up wasting most of her afternoon on Ted. Suddenly she grinned at her own reflection in the rear-view mirror. Not exactly wasted. Ted had been different and kind of fun in a strange way. It was a shame she wouldn't see him again.

It was late by the time she'd stopped at the cottage she shared with her grandmother, took a quick shower, and changed to her white uniform with its green apron.

Cars surrounded Dovie's Bayside Café, a modest-looking, white building, attractively landscaped with half a dozen palm trees and other tropical plants. The Bayside wasn't a fancy restaurant, but Stacy knew for a fact it served some of the best food in town. After all, Gran was cook.

The smell of good food greeted her as she rushed into the kitchen and hugged the round little person who was heaping plates with shrimp and French fries. "Sorry I'm late, Gran. Time got away from me."

"I'm glad you enjoyed yourself. Marti Sanderson called to say you and your friend had dropped by."

Word sure traveled fast! Stacy stared at her grandmother, not knowing whether to laugh to protest. Couldn't she make a move without someone's telling on her?

"I'm glad you had a good time, dear, but what do you think Dwayne would say?"

Her aunt breezed in from the dining room. "Thank goodness, you're here, Stacy. We have a mob out there." Aunt Marilyn, who was Gran's younger sister, reached for the shrimp plates. "Dwayne's out front. He's asking for you."

Stacy made a face, but she went out to the dining room without further debate. After all, she was lucky to be going steady with Dwayne.

He was sitting in the corner booth. She smiled and waved to him before going to take orders from waiting customers. By the time the rush had died down a little and she was able to turn her full attention to him, he was halfway through the cheeseburger her aunt had brought him. She sat down across from him.

"Hi." He smiled, showing even teeth that practically glowed against his dark, athlete's tan. Not for the first time, she thought he could have posed for a toothpaste ad—or even better, one for suntan oil. "A little late getting back?"

She nodded, feeling guilty for no reason she could understand. It was as if she'd really been two-timing him. "I lost track of time."

He shook his head. "Beats me why you wanted to skip a party just to go over to the island all by yourself."

Stacy picked up a paper napkin and began to rip it into thin strips. "They were your friends, Dwayne. I don't think they like me much."

"How could they, considering the way you always clam up when they're around. If you ask me, you're the one who doesn't like them."

This was entirely too true. "They do seem a little snobby to me."

He glared. "Do I criticize your friends?"

Confused, she heaped the napkin strips into a little pile. Six months ago when Dwayne first had noticed her existence, she'd felt as though all her dreams had come true. And when he'd given her his class ring, she'd padded it with tape and worn it on her finger, feeling like the proudest girl in the world.

What had gone wrong? Lately she'd started to feel as though the ring were too heavy for her hand. Maybe that was why she'd forgotten and left it on her bureau this morning. That was why she hadn't been wearing it when she met Ted.

Ted! Why did he keep popping back into her mind?

She drew a deep breath. "It's not that I don't like your friends, Dwayne, but they're older than I am and interested in different things, I guess." It was funny how she couldn't seem to come out with a definite statement these days. She was hesitant to speak her own mind. Dwayne was too apt to tell her she was wrong.

He got up. "That's probably it, sweetie," he agreed. "We've just got to build up your confidence." He looked around to make sure neither her grandmother nor her aunt was watching them, then quickly kissed her cheek. "Don't worry, you know I think you're perfect exactly the way you are."

Glumly she watched him leave, wondering why he was always trying to change her if he thought she was so perfect. She tried to think of excuses for him. Maybe it was because he was a year older and already in junior college. Or because his family was so much better off financially than hers.

Dejectedly she got up and began clearing the table. She'd have to watch out. She was getting too negative these days. Dwayne was a wonderful person: good-looking, bright, and full of ambition. People said he'd go places.

Aunt Marilyn came up to circle her waist with one arm. "You look tired tonight, Stacy. The crowd's beginning to clear out; you'd better go home and get a good night's sleep so you can be fresh for school tomorrow."

Stacy didn't argue, but smiled gratefully at her aunt. Aunt Marilyn and Gran were quite a pair. Gran was in her 50's while her younger sister was nearly 20 years younger, but between them they had enough get-up-and-go to fuel another person. The restaurant was their livelihood but they managed to have a good time running a business that some people might have considered drudgery. It certainly was hard work. Stacy's feet were already beginning to ache. "I do have a little homework."

It was only a few blocks to the little, light-green cottage she shared with her grandmother. She'd lived here as long as she could remember. Her mother had died when Stacy was very young and her father, devastated by his wife's death, had left his daughter in the temporary care of his own mother. Temporary had turned into permanent and though Stacy spent each summer with her dad in Houston, this was her real home.

The cottage was made up of a living room, small kitchen, a bath, and two bedrooms, one for Gran and one for Stacy. Aunt Marilyn had her own place, a mobile home in back of the café.

The little house was modest, but attractively furnished in light-weight furniture that suited the near-tropical climate. When she thought about it, she liked living here. Most of her life, she'd taken it for granted, at least until she'd been invited to Dwayne's beautiful estate. For a few days, she'd been envious, but then home started looking pretty good again. It might not be fancy, but as her aunt always said, at least it was theirs.

She had showered before going to the café, but now she took a long, leisurely bath, toweled dry, and then put on pajamas, slippers, and a robe.

She took her history homework and a cold soda and went to the screened porch that ran the length of the back of the house. She settled in her favorite sprawling chair and opened the textbook. But it was hard to think of homework when the air felt soft and warm, in spite of the fact that it was February, and the salt tang of sea air seasoned the night.

Such weather must seem strange to the boy from Chicago. He must be used to snow, cold wind, and heavy coats at this time of year. She wondered how he felt over there on the island with the wind from the sea rocking his van.

She tried hard to force her mind to a study of Greek civilization, but it wouldn't seem to settle there. What about Ted? What was he doing here by himself?

The ringing of the telephone summoned her back into the main body of the house. Dwayne was on the line.

"Just wanted to give you a call before you went to bed. I know how early you like to turn in."

"Not this early," Stacy protested, looking at her watch. "It's not even nine yet. Gran should be home any minute now. Why don't you come over and have a snack with us?"

"Look, sweetie, I'd love to, really I would . . . but I've got piles of homework to do yet. College is a whole lot tougher than high school."

"I suppose so." Stacy couldn't help being disappointed that he didn't want to come over. When they'd started going together last fall, he'd just been starting college, but now they didn't get to spend much time together. "But I wish you could come over."

"Maybe we can get together later in the week."

"Sure," she agreed. "Good night." She hung up slowly. If only he'd come over. Maybe his living, breathing presence would push the memory from her mind of a serious, gray-eyed boy on a sandy beach.

2

Stacy waved good-bye to a cluster of her friends and dashed down the sidewalk to the waiting yellow Camaro. "Sorry, Maria," she panted, climbing in beside her friend. "But Chris wanted to borrow my history notes."

"Hope you didn't lend them to him. He can take notes for himself."

Stacy grinned cheerfully. "I'll say no next time."

Her friend's dark eyes flashed as she glanced skeptically at her. "You let people take advantage of you." Her Mexican heritage tinged her speech with only the softest, most attractive accent, even though, Stacy knew, Spanish was the language spoken in her home. Maria was a third-generation Texan and proud of being bilingual. "Chris could take his own notes if he were willing to pay attention in class."

"I suppose." Stacy squirmed uncomfortably. She'd heard this lecture before. "But it's hard to say no."

Maria mumbled something unintelligible. "Want me to drop you at home or at the restaurant?"

"At the restaurant. Gran asked me to fill in for her this afternoon so she could go to the dentist." Stacy leaned back against the comfortable vinyl of the seat, trying not to feel envious of

Maria. Her parents had given her this beautiful car, but nobody in Stacy's family could afford to give her even an old automobile. Every penny she could earn had to be put away if she had a hope of going to college. She grinned again at her friend. "Talk about letting people take advantage. You're always taking me home."

"We're friends. Besides you do things for me, too, and, anyway, I like the company."

Stacy smiled as she got out at Dovie's Bayside Café. "See you later."

The little restaurant was virtually empty except for a crowded table of coffee drinkers at one end. Good! Maybe once she'd helped Aunt Marilyn get dinner started, she could put in a little time on her homework.

She found her aunt in the back, stirring the braised beef that would be one of the menu choices for tonight. "Hi! How's it going?"

"OK." Her pretty blonde aunt looked preoccupied. "I just sliced some ham if you want a sandwich."

Stacy nodded, piling thin slices of ham and Swiss cheese on whole-wheat bread, then putting it on the grill to toast lightly. She went over to peer out into the dining area. Someone had just come in the door. "A customer. Be right back."

She grabbed a menu, nodded a greeting to the little group of businessmen from the area who were enjoying their coffee and conversation. She barely glanced at the young man who was at the table in the back, thrusting the menu into his hands.

"Hi, Stacy."

For the first time, she really looked at him and, just for an instant, she couldn't remember who he was. She frowned. Someone new at school, someone she'd just met? Then she remembered, feeling slightly foolish. "Oh, hi, Ted. Hope you didn't get your van stuck again."

He shook his head. "I'm being more careful."

It was funny that she hadn't recognized him right off, especially considering that he'd occupied more than his share of her thoughts last night. Probably it was because she hadn't expected to see him at the Bayside Café. "Funny you should happen in here."

He shook his head. "It didn't just happen. When I took the shovel back to Mrs. Sanderson, she mentioned that you worked here."

"Oh." Stacy's face warmed slightly at the thought that he'd asked about her and then had come looking for her. The romantic fantasy died a quick death.

"I thought you might help me get a job."

"Oh!" Why was it that romantic things never happened to her? Maybe it was because she didn't look the part with her expressive face and unruly blonde curls. She'd always known life had destined her for a comedy role, not as a leading lady. "You want a job." How stupid! That was what he'd just said.

"Sure do. I don't plan to keep living in my van forever and I've got to eat. Besides I need something to do to pass the time."

"You could ask my aunt. Sometimes, she takes on extra help."

He frowned. "Your aunt owns this place."

"My great-aunt, really. She and my grandmother. Come on back and I'll introduce you to Aunt Marilyn."

She led him to the kitchen where a mixture of delicious odors seemed to sizzle in the air.

"I flipped your sandwich over," Aunt Marilyn said, without looking up. "It was about to burn."

"Thanks." Stacy went over to remove it from the grill, setting it to one side. "Aunt Marilyn, this is Ted Lorimer. He's here looking for work."

Stacy couldn't help thinking how pretty Aunt Marilyn was. She had blonde curls, too, but somehow the whole arrangement of her face and form came out differently. Now she looked like a romantic lead! Her eyes sized Ted up. "What kind of work, young man?"

He stood quietly. "Just about any kind."

"Are you a friend of Stacy's?"

"We just met," Stacy contributed hurriedly.

"I'm from Chicago. I'll probably only be here a few months."

"A snowbird."

"A what?"

Aunt Marilyn regarded him thoughtfully. "It's what we call the winter visitors, northerners who come down to avoid the cold."

He shrugged. "I guess you might put me in that category."

"Are you in school?"

He seemed to hesitate. "I graduated last year."

Aunt Marilyn folded her arms across her chest. "A bright young man like you should be in college or working toward some sort of career."

Stacy grinned. Trust Aunt Marilyn. She had spunk enough to lecture a complete stranger if she thought the occasion called for it. Trouble was she didn't approve of ambitionless young men. Most likely she wouldn't hire Ted if things kept on the way they were going.

"Maybe he just hasn't settled on what he wants to do yet," she suggested tactfully. "But you did say something about needing someone part time to help clean up."

" I did say that." Aunt Marilyn glanced at Stacy, then turned back to Ted. "We can't pay much. It's only minimum wage and probably you'd want something full time."

Ted smiled for the first time. It made his whole face look different, not so serious, but lively and full of fun. Even Aunt Marilyn couldn't seem to help smiling back. "But, of course, if you're interested . . ."

"It's just what I'd like," he said eagerly. "I need lots of time to think things through so a few hours a week will be just what I need to keep going while I'm here."

Stacy sat quietly, munching her sandwich without tasting it as she listened to them work out the details of employment. Every now and then, she went to glance into the restaurant's dining room, but no new customers had come in.

When Ted had finished filling out the required forms, he looked up at Aunt Marilyn. "When can I start?"

She grinned at him. "What about tonight? My sister had to have a couple of teeth filled today and she's not going to feel so hot. If you give Stacy and me a hand, then she can take the evening off."

"Sure." He grinned again. He looked at Stacy. "That'll be great."

The men out in the dining room were leaving so Aunt Marilyn went out front to act as cashier. She told Ted to clean up the table.

Aunt Marilyn came back first. "Seems like a nice boy," she commented thoughtfully. "I hope Dovie approves of him."

"You know she will, as long as he does a good job. You're the one who's hard to please."

Aunt Marilyn grinned at the accusation. "If it had been one of your friends, Stacy, someone you knew and could recommend, I wouldn't give it a thought. But when it comes to hiring someone neither of us had seen before he walked in here, well, it worries me a little. Something about the boy, though, I couldn't help taking to him."

"And you've always been a good judge of character," Stacy reminded her a bit nervously. She hadn't meant to mislead Aunt Marilyn, but it seemed a little pointless now to mention that when she'd said she'd just met Ted, she'd meant yesterday, not today. "I'm sure it'll work out."

Aunt Marilyn nodded thoughtfully. "Better get out front. The dinner crowd will be hitting soon."

Within 15 minutes, Stacy was very busy, chatting with customers, taking orders. She exchanged a word with Ted now and then as they passed. He was looking a little lost and confused

with the bustle, but she was pleased to see he was working hard.
She felt somewhat responsible for him, as though her aunt had
employed him because of her. It wasn't true, of course, but she
was anxious to see it work out. It would be nice having him
around.

Aunt Marilyn had called Gran to tell her she needn't
come in, but about halfway through the evening she showed
up. "Hello, dear." She gave Stacy's shoulder a pat as she went
by.

"Couldn't leave us alone for even one night," Stacy teased.
"Figured we'd run the business right into the ground."

"That's not it." Dimples deepened in Gran's cheerful, plump
face. "But I was sitting at home, watching television and being
bored to death when I realized my teeth didn't hurt at all and I'd
rather be down here helping out."

"Dovie!" A woman just coming in the door called. "Don't tell
me they've let you out of the kitchen for once."

Gran turned to grin happily at the woman who'd just
entered. "Hi, Marti, Fletcher. Yep, they let me out once in a
while."

Stacy greeted the Sandersons with open friendliness. They
were almost like family to her. "Hello, you two. Come in for
some of Aunt Marilyn's apple pie."

"That and her good coffee," Fletcher Sanderson assured her.
"Now, Stacy, what's this about you paying us a visit while I was
away. No fair."

She laughed. "Wasn't exactly a visit. I was there to ask a
favor."

"Marti told me she lent you a shovel so you could dig your car
out of the sand."

His wife touched his arm. "No, Fletch, it wasn't Stacy's car."

At that moment, Ted, who'd been clearing a nearby table,
turned to face them.

"That's the boy!" Marti Sanderson said, looking surprised.

Ted smiled. "Hello, Mrs. Sanderson." He nodded politcly, then went on to the next table, removing dirty dishes.

Mrs. Sanderson turned in confusion to Stacy. "I didn't know Ted worked here. I thought you said . . ."

"Aunt Marilyn just hired him this afternoon," Stacy explained hurriedly, not anxious to go into further details. More customers were coming in the door and she used the excuse of having to show them to a table to escape, conscious that Gran was frowning at her. She didn't know what she was feeling guilty about, but she did.

Dovie's Bayside Café was an informal family place where many of the guests were old friends so Stacy tried to tell herself she shouldn't make a big deal of it because Gran sat with the Sandersons while they ate their pie. She didn't doubt, though, that she was the subject of the conversation because every once in a while they glanced her way.

It was a particularly busy evening, but it seemed that everyone had come in at the same time because, a little after eight, everybody decided to go home. Only a couple in one corner and three middle-aged ladies lingering over dessert at the table next to them were left. There was plenty for Ted to do clearing up and she decided she'd give him a hand once she turned in the couples' order in the back.

The minute she walked into the kitchen, she knew Gran and Aunt Marilyn had been talking about her. They were standing together and Aunt Marilyn moved abruptly across the room to start slicing more ham for breakfast. Gran stood where she was, her gaze serious on Stacy's face.

She wasn't one to avoid an issue. "Marilyn tells me this Ted she hired is a friend of yours."

"No, Dovie," her sister corrected. "I didn't say that. Stacy said she and Ted just met when he came in here."

Stacy shook her head. Now she'd have to explain everything. "I didn't say that, Aunt Marilyn. When I said we'd just met, I meant yesterday, over on the island. I was just walking along when, out of the blue, this boy called to me."

Gran looked shocked. "A strange boy simply walked up to you and introduced himself. Really, Stacy!"

Stacy tried not to smile. Gran was the friendliest person in the world. Aunt Marilyn often said she'd never met a stranger. "Everyone is friendly over on the island, Gran. You know that."

"You can't be too careful," Aunt Marilyn hinted darkly.

"I would have ignored him, but his van was stuck in the dunes and I told him I knew where we could borrow a shovel and dig it out. So we walked down to the Sandersons and borrowed a shovel from Marti."

"She did mention that," Gran admitted, "but she seemed to think you were very good friends."

"We'd just met." Stacy couldn't help feeling a little annoyed. Gran and Aunt Marilyn tended to be overprotective, but they'd always trusted her. Now they were giving her the third degree. "Besides I like him."

"She likes him." Aunt Marilyn looked significantly at Gran.

"You liked him too," Stacy accused. "I could tell."

"We do need help, but now I'm not sure it's such a good idea."

"Why not? He's been working his head off all night."

Gran nodded. "He really has been doing his best, Marilyn. It doesn't seem quite fair to fire him just because of Stacy."

"Because of me?" Stacy asked, insulted.

Gran reached across to take her hand. She patted it. "Marilyn and I both think so highly of Dwayne, dear. We know how fortunate you are to have a boy like that interested in you."

Stacy pulled her hand away, stepping back. Why did she feel as though bars were closing around her? "I like Dwayne, too; that's why I agreed to go steady with him, but what does that have to do with me and Ted?"

"It's a very serious matter when you agree to wear a boy's ring, Stacy," Gran told her.

"It's a commitment," Aunt Marilyn added.

Stacy shook her head. They were very sweet and serious —
also very old-fashioned. "It only means that I won't date anyone
else while we're going steady. That's all."

"But who can guess where it might lead?" Gran said, looking
dreamy.

It was really funny, or it would be if it were happening to
someone else. "I'm only 16," she protested.

"I was just 17 when I married your grandfather."

"Things were different then. Girls married at a younger age."

Aunt Marilyn nodded briskly. "You and Dwayne should wait
until he's at least finished college."

Stacy froze with shock. "Dwayne and I have no plans that go
any further into the future than next Saturday night."

"Oh, we know, dear." Gran and Aunt Marilyn exchanged
a look of secret knowledge. "But who can guess what will
happen?"

Disgustedly, Stacy turned back toward the dining room. "I
need two fish plates. In the meantime, I'll be out front helping
Ted clean up."

Shaking her head, she went out to join him. Gran and Aunt
Marilyn were really strange sometimes. Gran had been a widow
for years and Aunt Marilyn had never married at all and yet they
were so incurably romantic. They couldn't seem to stay out of
her love life. When she was younger, they'd worried because
she didn't have boyfriends. Then they hadn't cared for the
first couple of boys she dated, and now they approved too much
of Dwayne. Sometimes Stacy thought she might even have
liked Dwayne a little better if they didn't like him so darned
much!

Though, of course, she was very fond of Dwayne. Otherwise
she wouldn't be going steady with him. She tried hard to convince herself.

Ted looked tired and dejected, she thought. No wonder, it
had been a busy evening and cleanup work was the worst part of

operating a restaurant. "Let me give you a hand," she offered.

"Thanks, but I'm about finished here."

She reached for a cup and put it on his cart. "It's not this busy every night. In fact, Mondays are usually kind of slow. I don't know why half of Port Isabel decided to eat at the Bayside tonight."

"I don't mind. Time passes quickly when you're busy. Besides I want your aunt to feel she made a good deal when she hired me."

Stacy glanced uneasily toward the kitchen. Right now, Aunt Marilyn was wishing she'd never set eyes on him, but there was no reason he needed to know that. "I'm glad you're here."

"Me too."

She leaned closer. "You could have found more interesting work than cleaning up at a restaurant. Besides there's lots of places over on the island where you could have gotten a job and been closer to the beach."

He grinned. "This was what I wanted."

"It wasn't because of me?" She wondered if she should tell him about Dwayne, but somehow it seemed a little awkward. She couldn't just pop out with, "By the way, I'm going steady." It seemed presumptuous.

"Of course not."

They were standing close to each other, smiling, she supposed, like idiots, when she heard the door open behind her.

"Stacy," Ted said in a very low voice, "a tall, black-haired boy is standing in the doorway glaring at us."

"Stacy didn't want to turn around like a little girl caught stealing candy. "Is he very good-looking?"

He shrugged. "I'm sure my opinion of that might differ from yours, but I'd say he was remarkably ugly."

Very casually, she turned around. "Dwayne." Smiling, she went over to him.

"Who was that?" He indicated Ted with a nod of his head.

"Ted Lorimer. He works here. Aunt Marilyn just hired him this afternoon."

He led the way to a table as far as possible from the spot where the other boy was working. "I didn't like the way you were acting with him."

Once she'd thought it exciting the way he got jealous when another boy showed her the slightest attention. Now it just made her tired. "We were only talking."

Aunt Marilyn came in to serve the couple in the corner their fish dinners, then she came over to greet Dwayne. "What can I get you?"

He didn't even smile. "I'm not hungry. I just came in to see Stacy."

"We're through the rush, Stacy. You can let Dwayne take you home now."

Stacy didn't budge. She didn't want Dwayne to take her home. She sat without moving until her aunt had gone back to the kitchen. Ted was working as though no one else were in the dining room.

Dwayne sat very still, his face grim. A month ago, Stacy would have been plunged into gloom by his expression. She couldn't stand it when he got mad at her. Now she just sat and waited.

"I thought it meant something."

Stacy traced a pattern on the tablecloth with one finger. "What meant something?"

"Going steady."

She'd heard this already earlier tonight. It had been a long day and she was too tired to argue with Dwayne. Besides he was on the debate team at college and was better with words than she. He always won. "If you don't trust me, Dwayne, then maybe I'd better give you your ring back."

"Just like that?"

She stared at him, trying to figure out why she'd been so happy last fall when he asked her to go steady. He was handsome, and even if Ted couldn't see that, there wasn't a girl at school who hadn't noticed. Maybe that was it. Everyone else thought Dwayne Miller was super wonderful, so how could she feel anything but flattered that he liked her? But it had to be more than that. She could remember going hot and cold when he spoke to her. She'd hardly been able to think of her own name. Where had they gone, all those wonderful feelings?

Right now, she just felt tired. "It isn't working any more, Dwayne."

"Because of that boy over there." He pointed. "Whatever his name is."

She hated it when he got mad like this, so angry that when he spoke his words came out sizzling, scalding her. "His name is Ted Lorimer and he doesn't have anything to do with this."

"Oh, sure!"

She sighed. "It's over, Dwayne."

"You can't mean that. You're just mad because I caught you flirting with another guy."

It was no use arguing. She reached down to remove the ring from her hand. It wasn't there! She'd forgotten to put it on again. "I guess I left your ring at home. I'll have to mail it to you."

He tried to grab her hand. "Come on, sweetie. You know you don't mean it. You don't really want to give me that ring back."

"Oh, I mean it." Angrily she jerked both hands away, folding them in her lap.

He got up, reaching over to give her a quick kiss on the cheek. "I'm going now to give you some time to cool off and decide you want to keep that ring."

She watched him leave, wondering at her own feelings. He might not accept that she meant what she said, but after weeks of trying to decide and worrying that she might hurt his feelings, it had come easily after all.

"You all right?" Ted brushed at the next table with his cleanup cloth.

She grinned. "I haven't felt this good in a long time." It felt great not to be going steady any more. She was free!

3

It was very quiet in the restaurant kitchen the next morning. Stacy, who had driven over with her grandmother the way she always did, ate her omelet silently, listening to the steady beat of Gran's wooden spoon as she mixed pancakes. It wasn't Aunt Marilyn's morning to work, but she was there anyway, dressed in a lime-green dress that made her look as pretty as the fashion models in the magazines.

"I'm not very hungry this morning." Stacy put down her fork. "Think I'll get started for school."

"A growing girl should eat a proper breakfast." Gran frowned, putting down her spoon.

"Besides you'll get there too early if you leave now," Aunt Marilyn added. She opened her purse to take out a compact, touching her lips with tangerine-colored gloss.

Stacy watched her with fascination. She seemed to do it effortlessly, yet her lips looked perfect, just as if nature had added the color. For Stacy, it always seemed to go on in one big blob and she had to work forever to get it to look smooth. She sighed. Some women just seemed to have a flair for looking terrific and Aunt Marilyn was one of them.

"Big plans for today?" she asked.

Aunt Marilyn shrugged. "Jonas is taking me into Brownsville to do some shopping, and then we'll have lunch." She smiled at her niece. "It'll be fun to eat in a really good restaurant for once."

"Marilyn Wylie!" Her sister waved the wooden spoon at her. "You may find a fancier place to eat than the Bayside, but the cooking won't be any better."

Laughing, Aunt Marilyn went over to give her older sister a hug. "I know it won't be, Dovie. Nobody cooks better than you—or I!"

Stacy watched them with a warm feeling. They were more her family than her own dad was. It was fun when she went up to spend the summer with him and Madge and her two little half-brothers, but this was where she belonged. Aunt Marilyn and Gran, exasperating as they were, were her family.

"I like Jonas," she said. "He's funny and interesting."

"And he knows it," Aunt Marilyn assured her. "A more self-confident man was never born."

Stacy grinned. It was true. Jonas thought he could do anything, but he wasn't vain, just sure of himself. A fisherman with several boats in his small fleet, he was a successful local businessman and her pretty aunt's most persistent suitor. Sometimes Stacy thought that if Aunt Marilyn had ever decided to marry anyone, it would have been Jonas. But, of course, now at the advanced age of thirty-eight, she wasn't likely to marry.

"I like Jonas too," Gran agreed, "but then the women in our family have always had good taste in men." Her glance included Stacy.

It was as good a time as any to break the news. "I'm going to school now," she said, picking up her books and heading for the door. "By the way, I broke up with Dwayne last night."

"Oh, no, Stacy!"

"What happened, darling?" Gran stopped what she was doing to rush sympathetically to Stacy's side.

She shrugged. "Not a whole lot. He just got mad about something. We had a fight and I gave him his ring back. Or at least, I will give it back. I forgot and left it at home again." She grimaced. "Anyway, we're not going steady any more." It was funny how good she felt just saying that.

Obviously Gran and Aunt Marilyn didn't share her feelings. They looked as if somebody had just died.

"Don't be too sad." Gran patted her shoulder. "These things happen."

"It'll work out, Stacy," Aunt Marilyn assured her. "Every couple has little disagreements now and then. A few days from now, you'll be back together and laughing about the fact that you ever quarreled."

Stacy stared at them in dismay. Why were they so determined to see her as Cinderella and Dwayne as Prince Charming—or maybe to update a bit, as Princess Di and Prince Charles. Well, perhaps she did have a little to do with that. It made her face burn to remember how she'd babbled to them a few months back about how terrific Dwayne was.

"It's no big deal. I'll survive and so will he. But we're not getting back together."

"Let me fix you some pancakes," Gran said. "No wonder you couldn't eat those eggs, but pancakes will go down better, or maybe some hot cereal."

"I'm not hungry and it isn't because I'm terribly upset or anything. Gran, I broke up with Dwayne. It was what I wanted."

Stunned silence greeted this announcement.

"I just wasn't ready to go steady. And I realized that when Dwayne came in and made a big fuss just because I was talking to Ted." Oops, she hadn't meant to tell them the part about Ted. They were bound to misunderstand.

"Ted!" Gran sounded startled. She looked at Aunt Marilyn. "That new boy you hired just last night? What does he have to do with . . ."

Aunt Marilyn shook her head, frowning slightly, and Gran stopped in midsentence.

"I guess I'd really better get to school," Stacy said for about the third time. This time, no one stopped her and once she was out in the street she could breathe a little more easily. But her elated mood was gone. Gran and Aunt Marilyn had spoiled it.

She walked slowly to school and was only about a block from Port Isabel High when a horn sounded from behind her. She looked up to see a flash of yellow. "Maria!" She lifted a hand in greeting.

"Hop in," her friend called.

When Stacy got in, the other girl flashed a smile that seemed even more dazzling against her perfect olive skin. "I went by the Bayside, but your aunt said you'd already left. She sure had on a great-looking outfit. She's good-looking for a woman her age."

"She was going out," Stacy answered vaguely. "That's why she was dressed up."

"A date?"

"No, not really. Jonas Barkley's just taking her shopping and out to eat."

"I think Mr. Barkley's really handsome."

"I suppose." Stacy shrugged.

Maria wheeled the Camaro into a parking spot and turned to her friend. "What's with you this morning?"

Stacy grinned weakly. "I broke up with Dwayne last night."

"Good for you! Congratulations are in order."

"I know you don't like him, Maria, but my grandmother and aunt do and they're very unhappy about it."

Stacy opened the door and reached into the back seat for her books. "So? You can't choose your boyfriends to please them." She grinned suddenly. "Or even to please me. That's why I've kept my mouth shut on the subject of Dwayne Miller."

Stacy couldn't help laughing. Ever since she'd started going with Dwayne, Maria had disapproved openly. She said he was a stuffed shirt. In the early days when Stacy had been so gone on him, it had come close to breaking up their friendship. It just showed what good friends they really were, she thought now, that they could keep on liking each other even when they saw things from such opposite viewpoints. "Your taste in boys is so different from mine."

"Good thing. It'd be harder if we liked the same ones."

Stacy giggled. "I guess. But you never could see Dwayne's good qualities."

"Didn't have any." Maria led the way down the walk toward the front entrance. She glanced at her friend. "Darned few, anyway."

"Everybody thinks he's good-looking."

"I don't."

"And he's intelligent."

"And he knows it."

"You're not being fair, Maria." Stacy nodded a greeting to a group of friends.

"And how come you're defending him if you've broken up? I can just guess what happened. He fell for some college girl and decided you were too juvenile."

"It wasn't like that at all. I'm the one who called it off."

Maria flashed a smile. "I like that! Must have set his self-confidence back a step or two."

Stacy glanced down thoughtfully, suddenly realizing what had been bothering her ever since the talk with Gran and Aunt Marilyn. "I've been worried that he's hurt, Maria. He really is more sensitive than you give him credit for being."

The amused look vanished from her friend's face. She beckoned Stacy over to one side where they could talk in relative privacy in spite of the crowds of milling students around them. "We've got five minutes before the bell. Tell me what happened."

"Dwayne came into the Bayside while I was talking and laughing with Ted."

Maria's black eyebrows raised questioningly. "Who's Ted?"

"A boy I met over on the beach last Sunday. His van was stuck in the sand and I helped dig it out. Then he came into the restaurant looking for work and Aunt Marilyn hired him. Now she wishes she hadn't because she thinks he's responsible for my breaking up with Dwayne."

Maria stared at her for a moment. "I thought we told each other everything."

"Oh, come on, it was no big deal, just a boy I met unexpectedly on the beach."

"But Dwayne didn't like it?"

"He positively exploded. Acted as if he'd caught us kissing or something."

"He's always been jealous. He likes to think of you as his personal property."

"Not any more."

The sound of a buzzer sent students scurrying down the halls toward classes. Maria shifted the load of her books from one arm to the other. "Come on! We'll be late and Mrs. Hazlett will have our scalps."

"Algebra II!" Stacy frowned in sudden horrified realization. "With everything that happened last night, I forgot to do my homework."

"Oh, Stacy, you oaf! You know how Hazlett feels about her precious homework assignments."

Stacy tried to smile. "Well, come on. Let's not add being tardy to the list of crimes."

Maria raced along at her side, trying to keep up with the taller girl. "You're sure getting off to a great start with this not going steady thing. You have to face facts, Stacy. You just don't handle emotional crisis well."

Stacy got off more easily than she expected in algebra, though the teacher did wear a pained look throughout the class at the thought that one of her most dependable students had failed her. Stacy promised to do the assignment during study hall and turn it in at the end of the day.

"Don't wait for me after school today," she whispered to Maria as they left class. "I'm bound to be late because you know Hazlett will want to give me her standard 20-minute lecture on the importance of homework."

"Your grandmother will be expecting you at work. Shall I give her a call and tell her you'll be late?"

Stacy shook her head. "She and Aunt Marilyn had a meeting last weekend. They decided I'm putting in too many hours at the restaurant, so I'm to take every other night off. Carol will be waitress tonight with Aunt Marilyn filling in if it gets busy."

"Carol? She's that dumpy-looking college junior."

"She's not dumpy exactly. I like Carol."

"Doesn't mean she has to be a beauty. Plenty of plain people have loads of friends. Just look at me."

Stacy laughed as Maria went sailing off down the hall. One of the things she liked about Maria was that though she was one of the prettiest girls in school, she wasn't stuck on herself.

Mrs. Hazlett fixed a stern gaze on Stacy. "I'll be expecting you right after school."

Stacy didn't have to try hard to look meek. The algebra teacher scared her to death. "Yes, Mrs. Hazlett."

She was pleased later that afternoon when the teacher responded more favorably to a completed homework paper. "Thanks, Stacy. I wouldn't have been so strict with you about this, but learning to meet your obligations is an important lesson in maturing."

Stacy ducked her head in an embarrassed nod. Maybe there were kids in the class who needed this lecture, but she'd always been responsible about her work. One missed assignment didn't make her a delinquent. "Something came up last night that made me forget."

The teacher sighed. "I should be able to identify with that. My own memory seems to be slipping these days. But at your age, Stacy, that's hardly a good excuse."

Stacy grinned. "Not an excuse, Mrs. Hazlett, a reason."

"I suppose you do keep busy," the teacher seemed to relent a little. "I understand you work very hard in that restaurant your grandmother operates. It must be hard to keep up your school work and do that as well."

Stacy bristled defensively. She was making it sound as though she were a poor overworked girl, which wasn't the case at all. The work *was* hard sometimes, but it was fun too. People were always coming in, friendly people who stopped to chat, and working with Aunt Marilyn and Gran was an experience. "I like working with my grandmother and aunt," she said, frowning a little. "The Bayside is a family business."

"I suppose." Mrs. Hazlett seemed unconvinced. "Anyway, Stacy, that's all for now. I'm exhausted."

Stacy picked up her books and prepared to leave.

"Do say hello to Dwayne for me, Stacy," the teacher called after her. "Tell him we miss him here at the high school."

Stacy nodded, not even tempted to explain that she probably wouldn't be seeing a whole lot of Dwayne any more. What was it about him that made adults like Gran and Mrs. Hazlett like him so much? No, that wasn't fair. The kids liked him too. He'd been runner-up for most popular boy in last year's annual contest. Maria was one of the few who didn't like him.

It wasn't that there was anything wrong with him, Stacy decided. He was fun and bright and he didn't kick dogs or anything like that. It was just that the more they'd gone steady, the more he'd taken charge of her life. It was just as Maria said—he seemed to think she belonged to him.

She straightened her shoulders as she walked out of school. She didn't belong to anyone but herself!

It was amazing how quickly the area around the school could be abandoned. A few kids still stood around out front waiting for rides, but the vast horde had departed. Stacy strolled slowly in the late afternoon sunshine, pleased to think of the evening ahead. As much as she enjoyed the bustle of the busy restaurant, it was nice too to think of having the hours ahead to spend just as she liked.

Not much homework tonight. She could call Maria and suggest they meet downtown for a movie. Or she might just pick out a good book and take a long, relaxing bath.

She'd walked about half a block when she began to have the feeling of being followed. She glanced around cautiously, prepared to dash up to the nearest door as though it were her home, when she thought she recognized the vehicle behind her.

She turned around. The battered brown van looked familiar and her last doubt vanished when a boy with golden hair leaned out the window. "Need a lift?"

"I already told you my grandmother doesn't let me ride with strangers."

"I'm a reliable citizen. I can give my employer as a reference."

Laughing, she went around to the passenger side to climb into the van. "I'm not sure Gran would give you that reference."

A frown puckered his forehead. "She did seem a little cool when I was in earlier. Didn't she like the fact that your aunt hired me?"

"It's not that exactly." Stacy realized it would be hard to explain without having to tell the embarrassing truth, that they thought he was responsible for her breakup with Dwayne. "It just takes Gran a while to warm up to people." This was a slander of her grandmother's friendly personality, but better than having to tell the whole story.

He nodded. "My mom is the same way, but once she gets to know you, she's the best friend in the world. I'll just have to show your grandmother how much help I can be around the restaurant."

"Did you work already today?"

He nodded. "I went in to help clean up after breakfast, then stayed on through lunch. Even waited on tables during the rush, though the customers complained I wasn't nearly as pretty as you and Carol."

She laughed. "I'm not on duty tonight either."

"I seemed to have heard someone mention that." His voice was carefully casual, but he grinned wickedly at her. "That's why I thought you might be persuaded to share my picnic." He gestured toward the back. "I have cold cuts, bread, cookies, soda."

"Sounds good," she stalled, mentally going through a list of reasons why she shouldn't go with him. Gran and Aunt Marilyn wouldn't like it, Dwayne wouldn't like it. . . .

The list stopped right there. What Dwayne liked didn't have anything to do with her life any more. "Sure," she agreed. "I'd like to go."

"Great! How about heading over to the island?"

"Sure, if you promise not to get stuck again." She smiled. "But you will have to take me by my house so I can change out of my school clothes."

They drove to the little green cottage. He waited on the front porch while she went in and put on some old jeans and a long-sleeved pullover. She knew from experience that the breeze off the gulf could be cool at this time of evening. Almost as an afterthought, she left a note on the kitchen table saying that she'd gone to the island for a picnic. Most likely she'd be home long before Gran, but it didn't hurt to play it safe.

It was a very different kind of day from the one on which they'd met. They drove across the causeway in bright sunlight and Stacy knew she'd need the suntan oil that she'd put in her purse. With her fair complexion, she always had to be careful about the combination of sun, sand, and sea or she'd end up with skin that was lobster-red and painful. She glanced curiously at the boy at her side. He looked as though he were used to spending a lot of time outside. Her fair skin would never take on that even brown tan though.

"How do you like our climate?" she asked, just because that was usually a safe topic of conversation with northerners.

"I don't mind June weather in February. My mom tells me they're in the middle of a blizzard back home."

She glanced around the interior of the van. He'd done some housekeeping since she'd last been inside it. His belongings had been neatly stowed away, she supposed. At least, they weren't in sight.

They drove silently through the heavily trafficked area of the island near the causeway. "Gran can remember when no buildings were over here other than a shack or two. She says when she'd come over with her friends, the only way to get here was by boat."

"No causeway. No big hotels and fancy eating places." He indicated the buildings along the beach with a wave of one hand. "Hard to imagine now."

"It would have been better like that," she said a little wistfully, "but everything changes."

"Everything changes," he echoed, his voice sounding funny. She glanced curiously at him. "Something wrong?"

He shook his head, not answering, but looking steadily at the narrow little road ahead. "I thought we'd picnic down around that area where I got stuck. Not many people down there."

His voice still sounded funny, she thought. She couldn't help wondering what it would feel like to be so far from home and family and to have something bothering you. Maybe she could help. "Something is wrong," she said impulsively. "Can I help?"

For a minute, she thought he wasn't going to answer. Maybe he thought she was just being nosy. "You're a sweet kid, Stacy."

"I'm not a kid. I'll be 17 this fall." She couldn't help feeling indignant.

"So you're still sweet. But I'm not going to bury you under my problems. We came over here to have a good time."

He parked the van over on the side of the road and reached in the back for their picnic supplies. "Come on," he said. "I'm starving."

4

Stacy piled ham, cheese, salami, lettuce, and slices of tomato on a roll and took a bite, chewing thoughtfully. She glanced at Ted. He'd looked so sad and serious that first day on the beach; she was convinced now that something awful was bothering him. She had to get him to talk about it.

"Have some potato chips?" He rummaged around in the bottom of a large bag.

"Sure." When he pulled out the chips, she held out her paper plate and he put some on it for her.

"You're a great cook."

He grinned. "Took hours of working over a hot stove but it was worth it."

"Before I know it, you'll be back in the kitchen helping Gran."

"Does your grandmother do most of the cooking? Or does your aunt help?"

"Aunt Marilyn cooks some, but she says there's no question but that she has to take second place to Gran. And Gran says it's my aunt's business sense that keeps them going. They make a great team."

He nodded. "I can tell that already."

Suddenly Stacy wasn't very hungry. She put her sandwich back down on her plate. Maybe if she talked a little about her own life, he'd feel free to talk about whatever was bothering him. And she had a feeling he needed to talk to someone.

"My grandfather died when my dad was 19. Aunt Marilyn was just a year younger. She said she was worried about Gran and what she would do about getting on with her life, about money too. So between them they cooked up the idea for a little restaurant and they've been involved with it ever since."

"Your dad didn't want to go into the family business?"

She shook her head. "Dad and Aunt Marilyn get along better at a distance. He says she's too bossy and she says the same about him. Anyway, he lives in Houston. He's worked for the water department for years."

"How come you don't live with him?" He grinned. "You don't have to answer if you don't want to."

"I don't mind. My mom died when I was just a baby and Dad dumped me with Gran to look after. It was meant to be just a temporary arrangement, but he didn't marry again for several years and by the time he did, well, I was used to living here. I do go up and spend some time with them every summer. I have two little brothers now. Tommy is four and Zack is six. They're really cute."

"I have a brother, but Sean is older than I am. He's in grad school now."

It was the first glimpse she'd gotten into his background. "Do you get along?"

"Oh, sure. We're good friends—most of the time." He grinned.

"I guess that's the way most brothers and sisters are. Of course, my brothers are more like, oh, like nephews or something. They're so much younger and we don't spend that much time together. Though Gran and Aunt Marilyn were even further apart in age. They were the oldest and youngest in a large family, but now they're very close." She stopped, realizing suddenly that her plan was failing. She was talking about herself, but he wasn't contributing that much. Still, he looked interested. He seemed to like listening to her.

He'd finished his sandwich while they talked. Now he reached for a soda and a handful of chocolate cookies. "Been spending a lot of time feeling sorry for myself lately. Guess I thought I was the only one with troubles."

"You mean me?" she asked, surprised. "But I have a great life!"

"You lost your mom."

"That was awful for my dad and for the rest of the family, but I was too little to remember. Gran has been my mom."

He nodded absently and she knew he was thinking of something else. He took a swig of the cola. "I'd hate to think I was one of those people who go around feeling sorry for himself."

"Doesn't mean you're doing that just because you're trying to work through how you feel about something. You must miss your family a lot."

"Sure." He stared out at a fishing boat gliding lazily across the horizon. "I miss everybody, especially Dad."

"You must be close."

"We were. He died last October just after I started my first semester in college."

The statement was made in such an emotionless voice that Stacy shivered. She didn't know what to say. "I'm sorry."

He took another swallow of soda. "Me too."

She couldn't think of a thing to say but just sat there, looking at him with troubled eyes.

"There I go, feeling sorry for myself again."

"Oh, no." Stacy reached out to touch his arm. He looked up to see the concern in her eyes. A slow smile spread across his face, warming her.

"It's just that it hasn't been that long and it was such a shock. He was a doctor and I'd always wanted to be just like him. But after . . . after he died, I couldn't seem to figure out where I was going. I just wanted to get away from everything and everybody. At first, Mom didn't think it was such a hot idea." He looked up to see if she were listening.

Stacy nodded, still clutching sympathetically at his arm.

"But Sean, my brother, talked to her about it. We'd been down here once when I was a little kid, the whole family. We had such a good time and I thought maybe if I came back, I could start getting my head together again."

"That was brave of her to let you go."

"I never thought about it that way. You're right, I guess. Anyway, I call home every few days and talk to her and Sean. That was the deal."

"It must be rough on you, losing your dad so suddenly."

"I miss him. Just seemed to lose my hold on things. Couldn't think, couldn't concentrate, had trouble keeping my grades up. Kept wondering what does it matter. When I'm not even sure I want to be a doctor any more, it's hard to put in the kind of work it takes to get there."

Stacy nodded. She could understand that. No wonder he looked so sad sometimes when he thought no one was watching.

He glanced at her with a sudden shy grin. "Now how come I spilled my whole history on you like that? You're a good listener, Stacy Whitman."

"I've been talking too. You've done your share of listening. In fact, I don't think I've ever known a boy who really seemed to pay attention when I was talking about something serious the way you do. Usually Maria is the only one I can talk to like that."

"Who's Maria?"

"Maria Hernandez. She's my best friend."

"Did you tell her about your fight with your boyfriend?"

She looked up, surprised.

He shrugged. "I could hardly miss the fact that the two of you weren't getting along exactly well last night. Hope it wasn't something I said."

"Oh, no. I did tell Maria that Dwayne and I broke up last night."

"Sorry, didn't know the fight was that bad."

"Oh, it'll be all right."

He reached across to touch her hand. "Could be the best thing. At your age, you shouldn't be concentrating too hard on one boy."

She glared indignantly at him. He was just like Dwayne. Just because he was already in college, he thought anybody still in high school was only a kid. "Look, I'm not that young. I'll be a senior this fall."

"Sure, I know, but I didn't like the looks of that Dwayne guy. He kept glowering at you."

"He was angry."

"Well, he didn't look at you the way he should have."

She giggled. "I never heard that it was a crime to look a certain way."

He jumped up, grabbing her hand to pull her along with him to the edge of the water. "I'll make it a crime. No glowering."

"I'm not even sure what that means. You forget that I'm not in college yet.

"Glowering? Well, I guess it means the way Dwayne was frowning at you with his eyes all squinted and his face red. He looked as if he wanted to grab you and give you a good shake."

"Probably he did." She felt a peaceful feeling steal across her as she stood at his side, absorbing the darkening blue of the tossing water in front of them. That deep blue seemed to stretch out until it melted against the edge of the sky. It was good standing beside Ted. She liked being with him. After all the storm and confusion of going steady with Dwayne, this was nice.

She hated to see it end. "It's getting late," she said. "I've got to get back."

"Right now?" He sounded as reluctant as she felt.

"I'm afraid so. I don't have a whole lot of homework, but what I have has to be done. One of my teachers wasn't too happy with me today."

Together they collected the picnic things and put them back into the van. They drove slowly toward the causeway. "Don't you ever get a little scared sleeping down on the beach by yourself?"

"Not scared exactly. A little lonely sometimes. Anyway, I won't be doing that any more. I've got a room."

"A real room? Are you sure you can stand it after sleeping next to the shore with the stars overhead?" she teased. "I was sure you were a gypsy."

"It's OK for a while, but a bed with sheets is nice too. And I like being able to take a shower whenever I like."

She laughed. "Some gypsy you are! Where are you staying?"

"I've got a job."

"Not another one!"

He laughed. "This one will only take a few hours a week. I'm doing some odd jobs at that motel down near the causeway. It's not the classiest place on the island, just a kind of casual, family-type place. Anyway they'll give me a room for doing some work."

"Hey, that's great. Sounds like you're really independent."

"My mom insists on helping, but I want to see how I can do on my own. It's part of finding out who I am and what I can handle."

She could understand that, but she couldn't help wondering how his mother and his brother were taking this. Gran and Aunt Marilyn would be frantic if she went off by herself like that. But maybe he was too caught up in his own hurt over his father's death to realize how they were feeling.

When he dropped her off at home, she said good-night and went inside without inviting him in. She liked Ted more than anyone she'd met in a long time, but she wasn't ready for a new boyfriend. He was just a friend, that was all.

The next morning, she got up early and had breakfast ready by the time Gran came into the kitchen. "How about breakfast for the cook?" she asked cheerfully. "Grapefruit, hot cereal, and toast. I even made some coffee for you."

Gran eyed her suspiciously. "What's going on? Don't tell me you're failing a class or something?"

"Can't I do something nice for you without your thinking I'm trying to butter you up? I just thought since you were always cooking for everyone else, you might enjoy a turnabout on your morning off."

Gran bit into a piece of toast. "Good."

"Anybody can make toast. Try the oatmeal. No lumps."

"It's delicious. Obviously you've learned to cook from an expert."

Pleased, Stacy began to eat her own breakfast. She knew why she'd suddenly thought she wanted to do something nice for Gran. It was because of the things that had come into her mind after the talk with Ted last night, what they'd said about both her family and his.

"I tried to call you last night," Gran said casually. "You must have gone out."

"I left a note, but it was still lying on the table when I got home."

"Can't read a note over the telephone. Did you and Maria do something together?"

"Not Maria," Stacy answered, somehow reluctant to mention her outing with Ted.

"You went with Dwayne." Gran sounded so pleased that Stacy hated to deflate her hopes.

"Nope. Ted and I went over to the island for a picnic."

"Ted!" The word was a wail of protest. "Oh, Stacy, he's not the boy for you."

"Why not?" Stacy asked, an edge to her voice.

"Oh, it's not that, dear, it's not Ted. But Dwayne seems such a wonderful boy and I know he really feels terrible about breaking up with you."

"How could you know that?"

"I'm just guessing." Gran sipped her coffee, her round face troubled. "You're still upset so we won't talk about that now. I promised Marilyn I'd remind you she's going to pick you up after school so you can drive out to the country together. She wants to pick up some farm-fresh vegetables."

"We did talk about it, but I didn't know she planned to go today."

"If you have something else to do, I'm sure another day will be fine."

Stacy shook her head. "No, it'll be OK. Tell her I'll be waiting out front."

That afternoon, she stood impatiently in front of the school, wondering where Aunt Marilyn was. It wasn't like her to be late.

A boy she knew called to her from a red Mustang just pulling out of a parking spot. "Need a lift, Stacy?"

She shook her head. "Thanks, Karl, but my aunt is supposed to come by for me."

She watched the red Mustang drive away, hoping her aunt would show up soon. After another five minutes, she decided she might as well give up. Obviously Aunt Marilyn had forgotten or something else had come up. She might as well head home.

She'd only reached the edge of the school property when she heard her name called. She looked up to find a tall, dark-haired boy waving to her from a green convertible. Oh, great, just what she needed right now!

"Hi, Dwayne."

He pulled up beside her. "Hop in and I'll take you wherever you like."

"Thanks, but I don't mind walking."

When he smiled, she could almost understand why all the girls were so crazy about him. "Don't be like that, Stace. Just because we're not going steady any more doesn't mean we can't be friends."

She couldn't help smiling. "I guess not."

"Then you'll let me drive you home."

She hesitated a second, debating. "Not home," she said, "but you could take me over to the Bayside. I have an aunt who has some explaining to do."

"How's school?" he asked as they drove along.

"Fine. No problems."

"You've always been a good student. You're going to do great in college, Stacy."

"Hope so." She couldn't help feeling stiff and a little uncomfortable with him. It was almost the way she felt last fall when they'd started going together. Only back then, she'd been asking herself all the time how a terrific guy like him could possibly be interested in Stacy Whitman. "If I go to college. I haven't made my mind up yet."

They were only a block from the Bayside when he drove over to the side of the street and stopped. "Can't we take a few minutes to go somewhere and talk?"

Stacy wiggled uncomfortably in the plush seat of the automobile. Why had she agreed to this? "I don't think we have anything to say to each other, Dwayne."

"Come on, Stacy," his voice was husky and he moved a little closer to her. "We can just take a little drive and talk things over."

"We've already said everything."

"Is that fair? I just want to tell you that it was all my fault the other night. I know I'm too jealous. Can't we just drive around a little and talk it over?"

It was hard to say no. When he was like this, she could almost remember the Dwayne who'd fascinated her so. "Well, just for a few minutes."

He drove on, but instead of turning in the direction of the Bayside Café, he took the road that led out of town. Neither of them said anything at first as they glided past the sparkling water that seemed only feet from the road, crossing the narrow neck of land that connected the town with the countryside. A little further on, Stacy stared out at the landscape, admiring the tall, skinny sentinel palms that guarded the Rio Grande Valley like lines of soldiers.

"As I said, Stacy, it was my fault and I'm really sorry. I know that boy who works at the restaurant doesn't mean anything to you."

"No, Dwayne, it wasn't Ted. He just happened to be there. But it isn't you either, not exactly. I've been thinking about this a lot lately. Going steady just isn't for me."

"You don't mean that."

"I wouldn't say it if I didn't. Haven't I always been honest with you?"

"Well, sure, but. . . ."

"We don't have anything to say to each other, Dwayne. Please take me back."

"But I don't know what I did wrong. If you'll tell me, we can work it out."

Embarrassed and uncomfortable, Stacy stared at the orange grove they were passing. What was going on here? Dwayne didn't act like this. He didn't beg a girl to go with him. He didn't have to. "I've got to get back."

"Now, look, Stacy, I'm trying to be reasonable."

That angry voice sounded more like Dwayne! She drew a quick little breath of relief. It was worse when he tried to make her feel guilty. "You know, Dwayne, what's wrong with you is that you've never had a girl walk out on you before. It's always been the other way around."

Without saying another word, he pulled over to the side, wheeled the car around, and headed back toward town, driving at a speed considerably faster than he had when they'd driven out. He looked about ready to explode.

She kept quiet, thinking about how they'd gotten together in the first place. It was a little hard to figure out, but she could see now that she was different five months ago from the way she was now. Shy and inexperienced with dating, she'd been tremendously flattered to have Dwayne Miller show interest in her. But now she was a little more sure of herself. And Dwayne, no matter how much he impressed everyone else, wasn't the boy for her.

In record time, he pulled up in front of the Bayside Café. "If you can't see what you're throwing away, there's not much I can do about it."

Stacy thought of several near-brilliant replies, but refrained from saying any of them out loud. She was fairly sure now that nothing about Dwayne really was hurt other than his ego, but she wanted to keep from stepping on that again. It was going to take him a long time to forgive her anyway.

He wheeled out of the parking lot, his tires squealing. Stacy shrugged, then went inside.

Aunt Marilyn and Gran were seated at a table with a couple of their friends, businesswomen who came in regularly for a late afternoon break.

Stacy nodded in reply to their friendly greetings. "What happened to you, Aunt Marilyn?"

"Why, nothing," Aunt Marilyn answered, looking puzzled.

Very distinctly, Stacy saw Gran nudge her sister. A flash of realization crossed Aunt Marilyn's face. Stacy frowned. What was going on here? She strolled casually over toward the table.

She waited for their explanation. "Oh, yes, I was supposed to pick you up at school," Aunt Marilyn said. "Sorry, but I forgot."

Stacy looked from one to the other. It didn't take a genius to figure things out. Aunt Marilyn and Gran had tried to play Cupid. "And since you couldn't come, you sent someone else. That's why Dwayne came by."

"That must have been it," Her aunt agreed a little too quickly. "I mean, when I realized I was going to be delayed, I asked Dwayne to . . ."

Stacy regarded her coldly. "I thought you said you forgot."

Gran looked at Aunt Marilyn. She glanced apologetically at their friends. "Stacy has been having a little tiff with her boyfriend and Marilyn and I tried to give them an opportunity to make up." Her attention went back to Stacy. "Dwayne came by, dear. He asked for our help."

The rat! How could he use her own family against her that way?

Ted came in from the kitchen. "Hi, Stacy," he greeted her. "Everything's put away, Mrs. Whitman."

"That's fine, Ted. You've done a good job. Since you're finished, you might as well call it a day."

"Why don't we go get a hamburger and see a movie?" he said. "If you don't have to work tonight."

It took a couple of seconds for Stacy to realize that he was, of course, talking to her. Then she felt a rush of pleasure that he wanted to spend the evening with her. "No, I'm not scheduled tonight. I'd like to go with you."

Gran started to speak and Stacy was afraid she was going to say that she'd have to work after all. Then she gave a little jump and Stacy knew that Aunt Marilyn had kicked her under the table. She smiled unconvincingly at her granddaughter. "Have a good time."

5

They had thick, juicy hamburgers and fresh limeades; then went on over to the movie theater, finding they were a little early for the first show. They went back to sit in the van, watching passersby as they waited.

"Why doesn't your grandmother like me?"

The question came so unexpectedly that for a second Stacy didn't know how to answer. "What makes you think she doesn't like you?"

He shook his head, a puzzled frown wrinkling his forehead. "It's hard to figure, but neither she nor your aunt seems to take to me. The minute I walk up, they start acting stiff and funny. They're a little too polite."

"It's not you exactly. It's circumstances. Tonight they were upset about Dwayne."

"Dwayne? What does he have to do with it?"

Stacy watched a couple about their own age stroll by. They were holding hands and looking so intently at each other that they didn't seem to notice anything around them. She sighed. "You've got to understand Gran and Aunt Marilyn. They grew up in a romantic age. They still believe in fairy-tale-type love stories."

"So?"

"They have decided Dwayne and I were meant for each other. They're really disappointed because we broke up."

He leaned back against the seat, closing his eyes. "I overheard you talking to Mrs. Sanderson about this on the island that first day. It's kind of hard to believe that adults would be trying to push a kid your age toward marriage."

"Not marriage. At least, not for a long time. You've got to see how it's been for them. They've worked hard most of their lives to keep their business going and they haven't had much time for anything else. They want something different for me."

"You're tolerant. I'd be screaming if someone tried to interfere in my life that way."

She couldn't help laughing. "Oh, we argue about it all the time, but it's hard to fight because they're so sneaky. Today Aunt Marilyn was supposed to pick me up after school. Instead she just happened to arrange for Dwayne to go by for me instead."

"Poor Dwayne!"

"Save your sympathy. He just doesn't like the fact that I dumped him instead of having it the other way around. I've heard by way of the grapevine that he's been going with other girls at college. *I'm* the only one who's been going steady." It was the first time she'd admitted this out loud. Somehow it had seemed a shameful secret, as if she'd failed in some way. "No, Dwayne isn't the problem any longer. I just need to get Gran and Aunt Marilyn to leave me alone."

He was thoughtful for so long that she thought he must have fallen asleep. "Ted?"

He opened his eyes. "Time for the theater to open?"

"Just about." She reached for her clutch purse.

He got out and came around to open the door for her. "Stacy, I think I know a way to get them off your case."

"What's that?"

They walked together toward the movie theater, approaching the small line that had formed at the ticket booth. "If your aunt and grandmother want a big romance, we could provide one for them. We could tell them we're going steady."

She drew her breath in such a sudden surprised gasp that she choked and started coughing. He pounded her gently on the back. "Stacy, what's wrong?"

She couldn't tell him that the only problem was that she was trying too hard not to laugh. Conscious of the others in the line gazing curiously at them, she stepped a little further away and whispered. "It's sweet of you, Ted, but I don't think it would work."

"Why not?" he asked belligerently.

She could hardly tell him the truth, that Aunt Marilyn and Gran were a little bit snobbish about such things. Always poor themselves, they had an admiration for wealth and achievement. They wouldn't be at all pleased to have her announce her interest in the boy they'd hired to do cleanup work at the café. "It just wouldn't work, Ted. Take my word for that."

They waited in line to buy their tickets, then went on inside to munch buttered popcorn and drink watery iced colas while they watched the movie. Once Stacy glanced up to find him watching her in the near darkness. "You're a funny person, Stacy," he whispered.

She grinned. "But you like me anyway?"

"That's probably why I like you. You make me laugh and I haven't felt like doing that for ages."

Good! Maybe he was getting past the first awful sadness of his dad's death. "I like you too," she whispered back.

After the movie, he drove her home slowly as if reluctant to say good-night. "How about a tour of the town tomorrow night?" he asked. "You really should show me around."

"I should?" she asked. "How do you figure that?"

"It's your duty to the Chamber of Commerce. I'm sure they want you to promote tourism."

"I'm really sorry to let the chamber down, but I have to work tomorrow night. Aunt Marilyn has a date with Jonas so I have to help Gran."

He looked so dejected that she couldn't help offering an alternate plan. "How about if I give you the tour Saturday afternoon if you're not working then."

His face brightened. "I don't start until six Saturday evening so I'll have plenty of time."

"Super! I can't wait to show you the old lighthouse."

He glanced toward that structure, plainly visible above the other buildings of the town. "I can see it from here."

"But I want you to see it up close. It's our local landmark."

"The Chamber of Commerce would be pleased with you, Stacy," he told her solemnly.

She laughed. "I'll probably get a medal."

They saw each other several times during the rest of the week, but seemed to have only a minute or two to laugh together or exchange a little talk as they hurried past each other at work. Most of the time, he was going off duty just as she came on and she began to wonder if Aunt Marilyn and Gran were deliberately scheduling them for different work hours.

If that were true, they'd somehow messed up because both Stacy and Ted had Saturday afternoon off. They met in front of Stacy's house at one o'clock to start their walking tour of the little town. They started out by walking along the bay. "This is Laguna Madre," Stacy told him. "The mother bay and the father island."

"Padre Island." He nodded, looking out to where the long causeway stretched to the island where he was making his temporary home. He led the way out to a short pier where a small boy was fishing.

"Catch anything, Sandy?" Stacy asked.

"Naw, not yet. I need to get some other kind of bait, I guess."

"This is Sandy Porter, Ted. He lives in the apartments down the block from our place. Ted Lorimer, Sandy."

"Hi, Ted," the boy said. "You like to fish?"

"Sure do, but I didn't bring my gear with me."

"Where you from?"

"Chicago."

"That's a long way off. You can borrow some stuff from me sometime if you like."

"Hey, thanks. I might do that."

They waved good-bye to the boy and strolled back toward land. "I used to babysit for Sandy," Stacy explained. "Until he decided he was too old."

"Seems like a nice kid."

"He is, but then we have lots of nice people here."

He grinned. "Is that part of the tourist talk?"

She tried to look indignant. "No! It's true."

They stopped for a cold soda at the same place where they'd eaten earlier in the week, carrying their paper cups with them as they walked. It was a beautiful afternoon and Stacy felt as comfortable as a lizard sunning itself on a rock. Something about the combination of the pleasant weather and Ted's presence made her feel good.

"What about this famous lighthouse?" he asked.

"We'll go over there now," she promised, heading in that direction. "It isn't a working lighthouse any more, of course, hasn't been for many years." She looked up to where it stood guard over the town. "But I like to think of dark nights when it flashed a warning to boats approaching dangerously close to the rocks."

He chortled. "You ought to write for television, Stacy."

"Who knows? Maybe I will someday."

"You could if you wanted to. I can see the fishermen on those boats now, leaning out to look for the light."

"So we both have imaginations!" They stood together looking up at the lighthouse where a small but steady stream of sight-seers headed up the steps approaching it. "I'm not sure that's helpful to a doctor."

"And I'm not sure any more that I want to be a doctor."

His tone had changed completely. It sounded so bleak that she was alarmed. Maybe she'd better wait a few minutes before showing him the lighthouse. "Tell me about it."

They found a place out of the flow of traffic and sat together on the grass. "I can't even remember when I became interested in medicine. It was just something I always wanted to do. Because of Dad, I guess."

"Is your brother going to be a doctor too?"

"No, Sean is an architect. Says he'll build my offices for me some day."

"Can't beat a deal like that." She'd hoped to make him smile, but he was staring at the lighthouse as though he barely heard what she'd said. "It must be wonderful to be a doctor and know you can help people."

"But none of them could help my dad."

So that was it! She drew a deep breath, wishing someone older and wiser than she were here to talk to him. Still they must have tried, his mother and Sean and probably others as well. Sometimes a person your own age had a better chance of understanding. "They must have tried."

"Sure they did, but it was a sudden, overwhelming heart attack. After all he'd done to help others, nobody could help him."

"And that's why you don't want to be a doctor any more? Because you can't always win?"

Anger flashed in his eyes. "You make it sound like a basketball game."

Slowly she shook her head. "I didn't mean to. And it must be the hardest thing in the world to be a doctor and know that some people you just can't help."

"I guess it is," he answered slowly.

"And I couldn't blame you if you didn't want to be a doctor because of that. It would hurt an awful lot."

Ted's expression was thoughtful as he replied. "But, Stacy,

you have to remember that you win lots of times, that there are people who wouldn't get well except for the fact that you're trained to help them. It must make up for the bad times to see the people who are healthy and well again because of your skill."

She smiled gently, reaching her hand out to him. He squeezed it, then grinned. "I'm working my way to figuring out what I really think, Stacy. Thanks for trying to help."

She nodded, tears coming to her eyes. She brushed them away with her left hand. "You're lucky even to have an idea of what you want to do in life. Here I am, ready to go to college in only a little over a year and I don't have an inkling of what I want to study. I envy people like you who really care about something."

He reached over to brush the tip of her nose with a quick kiss. "Stacy, love, I don't know what you'll grow up to be, but I'm sure it'll be something very special. You have a gift for reaching out and helping people."

It was, she thought, the nicest thing anyone had ever said to her. A little embarrassed, she got up, brushing wisps of grass from the seat of her jeans. "Come on, Mr. Lorimer. Time to get on with the tour." She waved a hand to indicate the lighthouse. "You're about to visit an absolute historic spot, the old Point Isabel Lighthouse—that's what the town used to be called way back, Point Isabel. I'm going to tell you some astounding facts."

His smile was warm as he looked down into her face. "Go ahead and astound me," he said.

Her pulse quickened. She swallowed hard. What was going on here? This was only Ted. He couldn't make her feel this way.

6

After the lighthouse tour, it was time to report to work. They went laughing into the café together. A burly man with sun-bleached hair sat at the table nearest the door. "Well, hello, Stacy," he greeted her.

"Hi, Jonas. Come in for dinner?"

"Thought I'd have some of your grandmother's chicken-fried steak." The big man nodded genially at her companion. "Don't believe we've met."

"Jonas, this is Ted Lorimer. He's working here at the restaurant. Jonas Barkley, Ted. He's a friend of Aunt Marilyn's."

"Your friend, too, I hope, Stacy. Feel like I'm practically your uncle."

Stacy grinned, barely refraining from making a remark about how he'd have to marry her aunt to manage that relationship. She shouldn't tease, she knew. She was sure there was nothing he'd like better than to convince Aunt Marilyn to marry him. "How's the fishing these days?" she asked instead.

"Fine. We've been bringing in some good hauls."

"We have a large fishing fleet here," Stacy explained to Ted. "Jonas owns several boats."

"You interested in fishing, Ted?"

The boy looked a little startled. "Can't say I know much about it, Mr. Barkley. I only got here from Chicago a few days back, so it's all new to me."

Jonas nodded thoughtfully, then took a sip of his coffee. "I could use some extra help if you'd like to hire on."

Stacy stared at him. Where had this come from? Last she'd heard, jobs weren't all that plentiful, not with times a little rocky in the Rio Grande Valley the last couple of years. Certainly employers didn't usually offer jobs to boys they'd just happened to meet. Her eyes narrowed. "Fishing is hard work," she said.

"I'm sure a strong young man like Ted here isn't afraid of a little hard work."

Ted glanced at Stacy. He, too, seemed a little uneasy. "Well, thanks, Mr. Barkley, but as I said, I don't know anything about fishing. The most I've done is use a rod and reel in a stream when my dad took me on a trip into the woods."

"No reason you can't learn."

"And I'll only be here a little while. It would be hardly worth your trouble to teach me."

Jonas reached into his pocket to bring out a billfold. From it, he extracted a business card that he handed to Ted. "Just in case you change your mind, you can reach me at the number on the card—if I'm on land." He got to his feet. "I'm going back to the kitchen to see what is keeping my steak."

"What's going on?" Ted whispered.

Grimly, Stacy watched Jonas's departing back. "Beats me," she said, though she had an inkling of what the truth was behind this unexpected offer.

"Working on a fishing boat would be quite an experience," he said a little wistfully, "but there's something funny about his just coming up to me like that. Anyway I like working here." He grinned down at her. "The company's so good."

She grinned back. "I'm glad you decided to stay."

As the night progressed, however, it looked as though they wouldn't get to see much of each other. As usual, Stacy was assigned to act as waitress in the dining room while Ted was made cook's assistant in the kitchen.

It was a busy evening with the usual Saturday-night rush. It wasn't until nearly nine o'clock when the crowd had thinned that Stacy got a chance to eat her own dinner. She stayed in the kitchen with her plate, hoping to get a chance to talk to Ted, but Gran sent him out front to do some cleaning. It was almost as though she were deliberately keeping them apart.

Aunt Marilyn came into the kitchen, sighing loudly. "Wow! Busy tonight."

"That's good," Gran said. "Maybe we can keep the old place going another month."

Aunt Marilyn pulled up a stool to sit near Stacy. "Remember the days when it really was that tight, Dovie, and we were struggling from month to month?"

"Sometimes it seemed from day to day. I never thought we'd make it."

"But we did." Aunt Marilyn looked around the kitchen with a proud air, reaching over to tap a huge stainless-steel sink. "We may not be exactly raking it in, but we're prosperous. The Bayside has become something of an institution in this town."

"I suppose so," Gran nodded. "And where does all this talk lead to, Marilyn?"

Aunt Marilyn grinned. "I think we can afford to put on more help, take a little time off now and then, particularly you, Dovie. You work too hard."

"Sounds like a good idea to me," Stacy agreed. "You're getting so you don't even know how to relax, Gran. Even when you're supposed to be off duty, you usually show up down here. This café isn't the whole world, you know."

A slow smile spread across her grandmother's face. "You two ganging up on me?"

"It was entirely unpremeditated," her sister assured her.

That word reminded Stacy of something. She had a feeling she knew about something that had been carefully planned out. "Funniest thing happened tonight," she said casually. "Jonas walked up and offered Ted a job, just like that."

Aunt Marilyn glanced uneasily at Gran. "He did say something about it," she admitted.

"Really strange, isn't it? I mean, I'd just introduced them and he offered Ted a job. That's weird in my book."

"Well, no, not really. Jonas just needed some help and I suppose he thought one of your friends would be dependable."

Stacy stared at her aunt. Did she look that gullible?

Aunt Marilyn shifted position uneasily. "Jonas was really disappointed when Ted turned him down."

"I'll just bet he was."

Aunt Marilyn leaned toward Stacy. "You should give that some thought. What kind of boy turns down a good job, with heaps better pay, just to work in some little café?"

"A local institution," Stacy reminded her, grinning again. "At least, that's what I heard somewhere."

"Stacy!" Gran tried to look stern. "Your aunt is only concerned about your welfare. We're afraid Ted just isn't the kind of boy with whom you should be spending your time."

"I like him. He's really nice."

"I'm sure he is," Aunt Marilyn said diplomatically. "But he doesn't seem to have any ambition, dear. He's not going anyplace."

Stacy felt her temperature begin to rise at the unjust accusation. She felt like telling them that Ted was ambitious enough to have made concrete plans for the future and bright enough to have been admitted to one of the most prestigious universities in the country.

Her mouth was open to say just that when she remembered

something and closed it again. Ted had told her his plans in confidence. He might not appreciate her talking about them, particularly not when his life was in such confusion.

"Yes, Stacy?" Gran encouraged. "You were about to say something?"

Stacy shook her head. "No, I haven't anything to say."

"Darling, we've only your best interests at heart." Aunt Marilyn reached toward Stacy, but she backed away, wheeling sharply about to go dispose of her plate. Her stomach felt tight and she wasn't hungry any more.

It was unfair. Gran and Aunt Marilyn were making this judgment of Ted based on superficial information. If they weren't so sold on Dwayne, then they could see Ted more clearly.

Gran came up from behind to touch her shoulder. "We both like Ted, Stacy. He's a very likable boy."

"Then why did you try to get him another job to get him out of here?"

A soft pink flush darkened her grandmother's rounded cheeks. "Oh, Stacy . . ."

"We were only trying to help," Aunt Marilyn interrupted. "Ted would make a lot more money working for Jonas."

"But he likes working here and the money doesn't matter that much."

"Stacy, I'm afraid money has to matter to most of us. When you're out on your own in the world, you'll realize that. Ted isn't a very practical person, not the kind of young man we'd like to see looking after you a few years from now."

Stacy's hands knotted into fists. "I plan to look after myself. Don't you think I can do that?"

"Well, of course, dear, but . . ."

"And you're wrong about Ted. He's a really special person and I like him a whole lot." Anger bubbled unreasonably inside her brain. She wanted to speak out in his defense, argue that they were wrong about him. But it was hard because all the information she could bring to his defense was confidential. She couldn't tell them about his father's recent death or his mother's trust that had allowed him to travel halfway across the country alone. She couldn't tell them how he felt about helping people or even how he'd planned to be a doctor. All she could do was tell them how she felt about him.

"He's a terrific guy," she said, feeling the words terribly inadequate. They were looking at her as though she were a hysterical little girl.

"Now, dear, don't get all upset," Gran soothed.

"You'll look at these things differently when you're older," Aunt Marilyn added.

They made her so angry. "I can tell you how I feel about Ted. I like him so much that I said I'd go steady with him."

The minute the words were out of her mouth, she didn't know why she'd said them. It was so stupid. She supposed it was because she and Ted had talked about it so recently, how they could pretend to be going steady to get Gran and Aunt Marilyn to leave her alone. But she hadn't planned actually to go through with it.

She whirled around, ready to retract the statement, to say she'd been teasing or something. Ted stood in the doorway, a mop in his hands.

He had obviously heard her announcement, but he didn't even look startled. His gray eyes had a look of amusement in them. "I see you decided to tell your grandmother the big news, Stacy."

Stacy turned slowly, feeling like a mechanical doll with unoiled hinges. Gran and Aunt Marilyn looked as though they'd been struck by disaster. "I didn't mean to say that."

Ted put the mop down and came over to stand at her side. "We thought it'd be fun to keep it a secret for a little while. It would be more special that way." He smiled at her. "Blabber-mouth."

Weakly, she smiled back. "You know me. Can't keep a secret. Always blurting out everything I know."

The silence from the other two was deadening. Stacy felt her heart hardening. This was really too much. They were still interfering in her life. They couldn't even let her choose her own boyfriends. Maybe they needed a little lesson. She would wait a moment or two before telling them. "Hope you forgive me for telling them."

"Oh, sure."

She didn't know how he was feeling. She suspected he thought of this whole thing as a huge joke. She felt weird and awkward.

Aunt Marilyn stepped toward Stacy. "Let me see your ring."

Stacy looked down at her unadorned hand. Aunt Marilyn was sharp-eyed. She knew very well Stacy wasn't wearing a ring.

"Oh, exchanging class rings really is just for high school kids. I'm thinking about some more original token for Stacy."

Stacy glanced at Ted with new respect. He certainly thought quickly. "Ted is a college man," she said. "He's so much more mature than other boys I've known."

So much for Dwayne Miller, even if he, too, was in college. She thought of the class ring she'd wrapped and sent back to him in the mail just a few days ago. Maybe when he got it, he'd finally accepted that she was a lost cause. At least, she hadn't heard from him lately.

"But you'll only be here for such a short time," Gran said. "So going steady with Stacy can't be a very long-lasting thing."

"These little romances come and go at your age." Aunt Marilyn sounded relieved at the thought.

Ted leaned back against a sink with a thoughtful air. "I'll just have to stick around longer than I planned."

He was quick. Aunt Marilyn and Gran were suffering, but she'd let them off the hook soon. And they did deserve it after the way they'd acted toward Ted.

She had opened her mouth to confess the hoax when Maria poked her head in the kitchen. "How about taking a break and having a soda with me, Stacy?"

"Sure, Stacy, go ahead," Gran said, obviously relieved at the interruption. "Oh, Ted, it is time for you to go home."

Ted nodded and went to put the mop away.

"You can have a soda with us, too, can't you, Ted?" Maria invited. "I've been anxious to meet you."

Stacy got the drinks and they went to sit in a booth together.

"I keep hearing about you from Stacy," Maria told Ted. "How do you like working at the Bayside?"

"It's a job." He shrugged. "I can't say cleaning is my favorite hobby, but I like working with Stacy—when I get a chance to see her." He grinned. "You must be her friend Maria."

"Oops!" Stacy looked at them with embarrassment. "I forgot to introduce you."

"I *am* Maria. I hope Stacy didn't say anything too terrible about me."

"Nope. Said you were the person she talked to about things that really mattered."

Maria looked across at Stacy. "We're good friends. I don't always approve of the boys she chooses, but I think she did OK this time."

Stacy bit her lip. Not Maria too. "Ted and I are just friends," she explained quickly.

Maria nodded. "Sure, that's why your aunt just whispered that you were going steady." She grinned. "I thought you learned your lesson last time."

Stacy made a face, then giggled. "We're not really going steady. It's just a plot to get Aunt Marilyn and Gran to leave me alone about Dwayne. They insist on believing that I'm dying to get back together with him."

"And you're not really going steady?" She looked a little disappointed.

Stacy shook her head. "Afraid not."

"Well!" Maria shrugged. "And I was just going to ask you to double-date with Rob and me."

"Rob Cooper?" Stacy inquired with interest. "Is he your latest?"

"One of them." Maria flashed a mischievous grin.

"What did you have in mind?" Ted asked.

Maria leaned forward enthusiastically. "Rob and I are planning to go over to Matamoros tomorrow afternoon. I thought you might like to go along."

"Matamoros?" He frowned as though trying to put the name in place. "Isn't that the town over in Mexico?"

"Just across the border from Brownsville. They have a fabulous marketplace where all the tourists like to go. You can pick up some great bargains."

"Sound like fun?" Ted looked questioningly at Stacy.

"I've been there lots of times," she told him, "but I'd like showing you around."

"Maybe I can find a souvenir to take home."

"No problem," Maria assured him. "You'll find lots to choose from there." She got to her feet. "I've got to go now. Mom said I had to spend the evening studying if I wanted to go out tomorrow, so I'll see you then. We'll meet you at your place, Stacy, at about one."

Stacy nodded. "See you then."

After Maria left, Stacy looked self-consciously at Ted. "Sorry," she said. "Didn't mean to come out with that going-steady bit. It just happened."

He grinned. "I did feel a little sorry for your grandmother and aunt. They looked as though disaster had struck." He shook his head. "I didn't know I'd made such a bad impression."

"It's not that. They're totally sold on Dwayne."

"And you're not." His grin faded into a serious look. "It's hard for them to realize that you're growing up and have to make some of your own choices."

For some reason, Stacy felt really down. The world seemed to have turned dark around her. "I guess I'd better go tell them the truth."

He reached out to grab her hand, holding her in place. "Don't do that, not just yet. Let them think we're really going steady. You can tell them after a while that we've broken up. I don't want to be mean, Stacy, but it'll just help them get used to the idea that you're the one doing the choosing."

"But, Ted . . ." She shook her head, feeling bewildered.

"It's going to be important for you some day. Do you want to have them pick out the guy you're going to marry?"

"No." She smiled, warmed by his concern. He really seemed to care about her. "We'll let them think about it for a few days."

They were sitting together, looking very much like a steady couple when Aunt Marilyn came up to them.

"I hate to interrupt this, but we need your help, Stacy."

Startled, Stacy looked around. While they'd been talking, the dining room had begun to fill. The other waitress was looking harried as she moved among the tables. "See you tomorrow, Ted," she said, jumping up.

"Sure, I'll come by your house in time to meet Maria and Rob."

She watched him leave, conscious of Aunt Marilyn's disapproving presence at her side. Her resolution weakened. She hated the thought of deceiving them. Perhaps she should tell Gran and Aunt Marilyn the truth about this going-steady thing.

"Aunt Marilyn, about Ted . . ."

"I just can't see your going out with a boy like that," her aunt interrupted indignantly.

"What do you mean a boy like that? There's not a thing wrong with him."

Aunt Marilyn shook her head. "You don't know that. He's a stranger who just came wandering into town, not in school and not interested in any kind of real job."

"He's kind and intelligent."

"He lives like a vagabond."

Stacy's mouth set in a grim line. She wouldn't tell them, not for a few days anyway. "You know, Aunt Marilyn, there's something I've been wanting to discuss with you."

"With me?"

Stacy had to work hard to keep from grinning. "It's about Jonas. I just don't think he's right for you."

"Jonas?"

"I don't like the way he combs his hair or the people he sees." She leaned closer to whisper as though confiding some dreadful secret. "I've heard he spends a lot of time with fishermen."

Open-mouthed, her pretty aunt stared at her. Then comprehension came into her eyes. She picked up a menu to swat Stacy with it. "You wouldn't be trying to tell me something, would you?"

Stacy laughed and Aunt Marilyn gave her a little shove. "Get to work," she said. "Hungry customers are waiting."

7

Ted and Stacy were waiting on the front porch when Maria and her boyfriend arrived. The muscular captain of the football team was well-known to Stacy although not one of her particular friends. She introduced him to Ted.

"This is Rob Cooper, Ted," she said. "Ted Lorimer."

The two boys seemed to take an instant liking to each other in spite of their dissimilar interests. They talked football during the drive to Brownsville until Stacy was so thoroughly bored with the subject that she looked pleadingly at Maria.

Maria didn't bother being tactful. "If I hear one more word about recruiting or who the best player in Texas is, I'm going to dump the two of you, and Stacy and I will go to the market alone."

"Sorry," Rob said a little sheepishly. "Guess we did get to talking football a little too much."

"A little!" Maria eyed him sternly.

In the back seat, Ted reached over to wrap an arm around Stacy, pulling her to his side. "If we promise not to mention another word on the subject, may we still go with you?"

Stacy pretended to consider. "If you're sure you can behave."

They laughed and talked together, getting better acquainted, as they drove through Brownsville and across the international bridge into Mexico. They were waved on by the border guards and drove carefully through the narrow, picturesque streets of the old town. Stacy pointed out wrought-iron balconies hanging from the second stories of the graceful Mexican homes. It seemed to be a city of flowers with brightly colored blossoms glowing everywhere.

Rob parked the car and they walked together the few blocks to the market. Small boys darted past them, shouting to them in Spanish, and a steady stream of tourists flowed around them.

"What do you think?" she asked Ted.

"Colorful and different. It's hard to believe you can go just a few miles and feel you're in an exotic, foreign place." He grinned at her. "But then your part of the country already seems foreign compared to mine."

"And I'd probably find Chicago strange." She couldn't help thinking how much more he smiled these days; at that first meeting, he'd seemed so serious.

That thought stimulated another, less pleasant one. If he were getting better, then he'd probably be going home soon. She was surprised at how that thought stabbed her. She would miss him a lot.

"What's wrong, Stacy?"

He was looking at her with such concern that it made her heart do a flip, at least that was the way it felt. "Nothing's wrong. I just hope you're having a good time."

"Sure I am. I can't wait to tell Sean about this place."

"Who's Sean?" Maria called from just behind them.

"He's Ted's brother."

"Older or younger?"

"He's older," Ted turned to tell her. "Twenty-four."

"Lucky you." Maria made a face. "I have a little brother and a little sister. It's a fate worse than death, I assure you."

Laughing, they approached the busy, crowded market where everything from candies to perfume was being sold in heated exchanges. After strolling through the booths for a while, Ted selected an ornately carved chess set for his brother and a hand-woven shawl for his mother. Then he spotted the huge straw hats at the next stall.

"We've got to have hats," he told her. "Then we'll look like natives."

"We'll look exactly like all the other tourists," she told him with a giggle. "But if that's what you want, we'll get them."

After she had let him buy her an enormous sombrero and one for himself, they put them on and continued walking. She glanced around, trying to locate Maria and Rob. "We seem to have lost our companions," she told him.

"I'm sure they can find their way."

"They're not the ones I'm worried about. We are."

He circled her shoulders with his arm. "Don't worry, Stacy. I'll look after you."

She liked the feeling of his arm around her, it felt warm and cozy. She could almost imagine that they really were going steady. They seemed to belong together.

Even the vendors in the booths seemed to sense it and she caught more than one indulgent smile sent in their direction.

"A beautiful necklace for the pretty señorita in the blue dress," called a young man who looked to be no older than they were.

Ted looked at him. "A great bargain," the young salesman encouraged.

"Want a necklace, Stacy?" Ted looked down at her.

"It's very pretty, but, no, thanks." She shook her head. She started to walk on, but Ted didn't move. He was looking past the vendor to his displays of jewelry.

"You should have something."

She raised her eyebrows. "Why should I have something?"

"To remember me."

Again the awful thought penetrated her mind that he would be going away soon. Her smile was unsteady. "I'm not likely to forget you, Ted."

He was examining a tray of rings. "I like this." He selected a delicate little ring with a setting of dark, smoky-looking onyx. "It looks like your size."

He held it out and she placed her hand in his so he could slip it on. "Does it fit?" he asked eagerly.

"It's OK, Ted, but you don't have to buy it for me."

"I want to." He looked at the vendor. "How much?"

Inwardly she sighed. This was not the way to bargain in the market. The young vendor would be disappointed. He liked to make his customers feel they'd bested him after a good fight, she knew. "Twenty-five American dollars," he said, matter-of-factly, his voice dull.

This time, she sighed out loud. "Too much." She put it back on the tray.

"But, Stacy!" Ted protested.

She turned as though to walk away.

"Twenty-three dollars," the boy called after her. "A very good price."

Finally a glimmer of understanding showed in Ted's face. "I really like that ring, Stacy, but $23 . . . ." He shook his head.

"All right! Twenty dollars, but that's my absolute low offer and I won't be making a cent of profit."

Ted looked at Stacy and she nodded. He paid for the ring and put it on her hand.

The vendor grinned at them. "I'm only letting you have it at a bargain rate because you're such a nice-looking couple."

As they strolled on, Ted leaned close to her to whisper. "I feel a little guilty about bargaining him down like that. What if he really needed the money?"

"Don't feel too guilty," Stacy whispered back. "If you look in the stall down on the corner, they have similar rings for several dollars less."

"Oh!" He looked so taken aback that she tucked her hand into his. "But I like the one you bought me better. I'll keep it always."

He smiled down at her. "It can be our 'going-steady' ring. You can show it to your aunt as evidence."

The thought wiped the smile from her face. Suddenly she felt tired and a little lost in the cheerful marketplace. She looked down at the ring that now glittered on her finger and knew what was wrong. She didn't want it to be a fake, a show put on for Gran and Aunt Marilyn. She wanted Ted's ring to be on her finger for real.

When had this happened? When had she begun to fall in love with him?

"There are Maria and Rob," he said, pointing ahead. They moved swiftly through the crowd to join the other couple.

"About ready to head for home?" Rob asked. "It's getting late."

Stacy nodded so hard that she felt the sombrero sway on her head. "I'm ready to leave."

"Me, too," Maria complained. "My feet hurt."

At the border, they stopped to show the guard their purchases, then were sent on across the bridge. "What did you think of Mexico?" she asked Ted, trying to regain her cheerful feeling of earlier in the day.

"It's super, though some day I'd like to travel a little further than just across the border."

"We went to Mexico City last summer," Maria told him. "I have an aunt and uncle living there. It's a very interesting city."

Stacy listened as the other three discussed the neighboring country, and Ted even got Maria to teach him a few words of Spanish.

She was so tired that she could only sit silently, anticipating the moment when she could say good-night and go inside to the privacy of her own house. She'd take a shower and go to bed early. Maybe a night's sleep would help her shake off this dejected feeling.

Ted seemed a little reluctant to part company with her. He lingered on the front porch even after Rob's car had vanished down the street. "Wouldn't you like to go get something to eat?"

She shook her head. "I'm tired and I have a million things to do."

He grinned. "Like washing your hair?"

"What?" She frowned up at him.

"Never mind." He reached out to touch her chin with one finger. "See you later, Stacy."

She watched him get into his van and drive away, then turned to go inside. A light shone from the living room, but she didn't think anything about that. Gran often left a light on when she knew Stacy would be coming in alone after dark. But when she got inside, she found Aunt Marilyn sitting in Gran's big chair, staring at the television screen.

She frowned. "What are you doing here?"

"It's my sister's house. She says I'm always welcome."

Stacy laughed. "That's not what I meant. I was just surprised to see you sitting there doing nothing. It's out of character."

"I'm watching television," Aunt Marilyn informed her, rubbing her hands together in an unconscious gesture. "That's doing something."

Quickly Stacy stepped in front of the television, blocking the screen. "Tell me what you were watching."

"It was something about a boy and a motorcycle or was it a bike . . . ." She stopped and laughed. "OK, you win. I haven't a clue as to what was on."

Stacy plopped down on the sofa. "So what's going on and how come you're sitting there doing nothing?"

"I was waiting for you."

Stacy straightened up. "Is something wrong? Gran's not sick or anything?"

"Nothing like that. It's just that I have something to tell you."

"So tell." Stacy stared at her aunt. This was weird. Aunt Marilyn didn't act like this. When she had something to say, she went straight to the point instead of hedging around like this. "Come on."

Aunt Marilyn rubbed her hands together again as though putting on lotion. She glanced around the room. "I've always loved this house," she said. "Dovie has made it so homey."

Stacy nodded. "I like it too."

She waited. Aunt Marilyn got up to go look out the window. Since it was dark outside, Stacy was fairly sure she couldn't see much. "What is it? Don't tell me you've robbed a bank or something."

Aunt Marilyn turned, laughing. "It's nothing like that. In fact, it's good news." She drew a deep breath. "Stacy, I'm getting married."

Stacy blinked. She tried to find her voice. "Married! You?"

"That's right. Jonas finally got me to say yes. We're going to be married very soon."

Stacy couldn't take it in. As far back as she could remember, it had been just the three of them, Gran, Aunt Marilyn, and her. And now this was happening. "But you're too old! I mean, after you'd waited so long, I thought you'd never get married." She stretched an apologetic hand toward her aunt. "It's not that you're old, Aunt Marilyn, but. . . ."

"But 38 seems ancient when you're only 16. I understand that, Stacy. But I don't feel old. I feel young and excited about the future."

What Stacy was feeling was that too much was happening all of a sudden. She'd liked her life the way is was. Aunt Marilyn might not have lived in the same house with them, but she was family and now she was going to have someone else in her life.

"What's wrong, Stacy? I thought you liked Jonas."

"Oh, I do. He's really nice. I just never thought of him as your husband."

Aunt Marilyn smiled. "He'll be your uncle."

Stacy nodded. Jonas probably already knew about this when he'd said he felt like her uncle. He hadn't been joking. She forced her mouth to stretch into a smile. "I hope you'll both be happy."

"I'm sure we will, Stacy." Aunt Marilyn's tense posture relaxed and a glowing look of happiness came into her eyes. "We've waited a long time to take this step, but we feel ready for it now."

Stacy wished she could be as sure. She felt as though her aunt were leaping off the edge of a cliff. Maybe she needed someone to talk sense to her. "Why didn't you ever marry before?"

"It's hard to say. I was busy helping your grandmother get the business started and then keeping it going. I've always loved managing the Bayside. And then I had you and Dovie." She reached over to touch Stacy's hand. "You've been almost like my own little girl. I suppose that's part of it, seeing you grow up and knowing you'll be going off to college and busy with your own life before long now."

"You can't get married just because of something like that!" Stacy said, horrified at the idea.

Aunt Marilyn laughed so hard that little crease lines showed around her eyes. "Not just because of it, hon. I've discovered I love Jonas and want to spend my life with him."

"Took you long enough," Stacy grumbled.

Aunt Marilyn smiled. "Some people catch on more slowly than others."

"Jonas has been trying to talk you into it for ages."

She nodded. "That's part of it, I suppose. I love his loyalty and I like the way he feels about me. But I finally had to come to terms with how I really felt about him."

"And you love him? You're absolutely sure?"

Aunt Marilyn nodded, laughing again. "What is this, the third degree? Do you want me to take a lie-detector test?"

It wasn't funny. "I just want to be sure you know what you're doing."

Just as Aunt Marilyn broke into laughter again, the front door opened and Gran came in. "Everything's closed up for the night," she announced cheerfully. She looked questioningly at her sister. "Did you tell her?"

Grumpily, Stacy decided everyone had been in on the secret but her. Why did they treat her like a child? "She told me, unless you're talking about something else I don't know about. You're not planning to get married too?"

Gran laughed, but Aunt Marilyn didn't seem to think it was funny. "It could happen. It's been a long time since Lawrence died, Dovie."

Gran just kept on laughing, but Stacy, shocked at her aunt's words, stared at her grandmother with new eyes. Gran was many years older than Aunt Marilyn. Surely she wouldn't go off the deep end too!

"Isn't it wonderful?" Gran asked her now. "We're going to have such fun planning the wedding."

"I wanted something small and simple, just the two families," Aunt Marilyn confided. "But Jonas wants a real occasion so we've got our work cut out for us."

"Don't know why he should get what he wants," Stacy muttered, but they didn't hear her.

"I used to have an old recipe for wedding cake that belonged to my grandmother," Gran said. "Let me see if I can find it." She went off toward the kitchen and Stacy was left alone with her aunt.

"Truly, I do hope you'll be happy, Aunt Marilyn. I think Jonas is lucky to get you to marry him."

Aunt Marilyn smiled. "I'm the lucky one. And I've always been happy, Stacy, with my work and my life, but this—well, it's just more."

"I guess."

"Don't think this changes anything as far as you and I are concerned, Stacy. It doesn't."

Stacy tried to smile. Of course it did. Jonas had only been on the fringes of their lives so far, but now he would be moving in, edging her out of the way. Aunt Marilyn wouldn't belong just to her and Gran. She knew she was being jealous and hateful, but though she could pretend otherwise, it was the way she was feeling inside. She wanted everything to stay the way it always had been. "Will you still work at the Bayside?"

"Certainly! I'd never give it up. I've told you how I love it. But Dovie and I have already been making arrangements to hire more help. The time has come in our lives when we want to have a few moments for something other than work."

So things were changing already.

Stacy got up. "I'll go make some hot chocolate," she said, "and we can celebrate."

She passed Gran, who was carrying a recipe file, as she went into the kitchen. As she prepared the chocolate, she listened to the sounds from the living room. They were so thrilled and full of plans that she felt outside their joy, locked away by herself.

When the phone rang, she hurried to answer it.

"Stacy? Is that you? You sound funny."

She cleared her throat. "Hi, Ted. I'm OK."

"I just wanted to tell you what a good time I had this afternoon. What did your family say about your ring?"

"They haven't said anything. I haven't shown it to them yet."

"Oh." He sounded disappointed. "Well, let me know when the fireworks go off. Anyway, this afternoon was lots of fun. I thought we might do something together tomorrow night."

She swallowed hard, her interest finally caught. Ted was asking her out, almost as if it were a real date instead of just a game they were playing for others. "I have to work tomorrow night," she said, hoping he'd suggest another night.

"How about Tuesday then?"

"Tuesday would be fine. I'd love to go out with you, Ted."

He said good-night and she hung up slowly, caught in a lovely, dazed feeling. This was the last thing she'd expected. Ted had asked her for a date!

"Stacy?" Gran came in. "Aren't you going to come help us plan the wedding?"

"I was just heating milk for the chocolate." As she turned toward the range, the phone rang again. She reached for the receiver while Gran went to take the milk off the stove and mix in chocolate and sugar.

"Hello," she said, almost hoping it was Ted again. Maybe he had thought of something else he wanted to tell her.

"Is this Stacy Whitman?" a crisp feminine voice asked.

"Yes, it is."

"Stacy, dear, this is Marcella Miller. Dwayne's mother. Do you remember me?"

"Of course, Mrs. Miller." Gran turned to stare at her at the mention of the name. "I remember you."

"Well, dear, it's just been ages since we've been able to visit, so I thought you might join us for a little family dinner tomorrow night. Jan is home for a few days and I know she'll enjoy chatting with you."

Jan was Dwayne's older sister. She was married and had a baby, so Stacy couldn't imagine what they'd find to talk to each other about. "That's really lovely of you, Mrs. Miller, to invite me, but I'm afraid I have to work tomorrow night."

Gran shook her head violently. "Don't be silly," she whispered loudly. "We'll get Carol to replace you. Go ahead and accept."

Stacy shook her head violently, covering the mouthpiece with one hand. "I don't want to go. Dwayne has set this up. I know he has."

"Stacy?" She heard Mrs. Miller's voice. "Surely you can arrange something. We'd simply love to have you."

"You can't disappoint the Millers," said Gran. "You know you like them."

"They're OK," Stacy agreed, "but I don't want to go because of Dwayne."

"One evening won't kill you. Say yes."

Stacy hardly knew what she was doing. "I suppose something could be worked out, Mrs. Miller."

"That's lovely, dear. Dwayne will pick you up at about seven."

Numbly Stacy listened to the click that meant the other party had hung up. Then she turned to glare at Gran.

Her grandmother smiled sweetly. "Don't worry, Stacy. You can work Tuesday night instead."

8

Gran made her dress up for the dinner. Stacy put on her new blouse and lilac skirt, brushed her hair, and put on coral lip gloss. She had no choice but to go through the motions even though she dreaded this evening.

Several times during the day, she'd considered calling Mrs. Miller and canceling. But the thought of what Gran would say had kept her from it.

Besides, maybe her grandmother was right. It wouldn't kill her to sit through an evening at the Miller house just to please Dwayne's family. They really were fine people. But she couldn't kid herself about the motivation for this evening. There was no question but that Dwayne had put his mom up to it.

"Stacy, Dwayne's here," Gran called from the front of the house. Stacy gave her hair one last touch with the brush, made a face at herself in the mirror, and went out to meet him.

He held out a cluster of rosebuds. "For you," he said, being gallant.

Stacy was more aware of Gran's pleased smile than she was of the expression on Dwayne's face as he pinned the corsage on her shoulder. "Don't forget, Gran," she ordered. "This is your night off. You are not to drop by the restaurant just to check on things and then stay to spend the evening working."

Dimples deepened in Gran's cheeks. "I'll try to remember. You two have a good time."

"Oh, we will," Dwayne assured her, ushering Stacy out of the house.

She settled uneasily into place in his sports car. "I don't want you to get the wrong idea about my going to your house tonight, Dwayne."

"Wrong idea?" he asked politely.

She frowned at him. "I'm only going because I didn't want to be rude to your mother and because Gran insisted."

He patted her shoulder. "We're just good friends, Stacy. No reason good friends can't eat dinner together."

She eyed him suspiciously. "If you're sure that's the way it is."

He started the car. "Sure it is." He talked cheerfully as they drove out to his parents' home, telling her about college and what he was doing. She relaxed in spite of herself, reminded again of how interesting and charming he could be when he tried.

The dinner at the Miller home, a gracious adobe dwelling overlooking the bay, turned out to be a party that included a couple of Jan's friends as well as several relatives. Stacy felt uncomfortable at first, but soon was made to feel at home.

"Good to see you again, Stacy," Dwayne's dad greeted her with open warmth.

"Oh, yes, Stacy, dear. It's so good to see the two of you together again."

Stacy smiled uncomfortably at Mrs. Miller, feeling as though she were there under false pretenses. After dinner, she and Dwayne strolled out together to the orange grove on one side of the house. The sweet scent of orange blossoms was in the air.

"I hear your aunt is getting married," he said.

She nodded. "To Jonas."

"That's good. I always thought they belonged together."

"I guess."

"You don't sound too happy about it."

"Takes a little getting used to, but I'll adjust. I just never thought Aunt Marilyn would get married."

"It was a surprise. I ran into Jonas downtown. He sure seems happy."

"Aunt Marilyn does too," Stacy admitted grudgingly.

He picked a bloom from a nearby tree, studying it as though it were an unfamiliar object. "What went wrong with us, Stacy?"

She shrugged. "Just one of those things."

"That's no answer."

She smiled, looking directly into his dark-brown eyes. This was the Dwayne she remembered, the one she'd been so pleased to have as a steady.

"Was it because you heard that I'd been kind of dating some other girls?"

"How do you 'kind of' date?"

He laughed a little sheepishly. "I didn't plan to be dishonest about it. It just happened. But you were the one who mattered all the time."

"Maybe that's what went wrong, Dwayne. We just weren't ready to concentrate exclusively on each other. There's nothing wrong with wanting to go with other people, but I'd have liked it better if you'd come out and told me that's how you felt."

"But I didn't feel that way. I didn't want you to go with other boys."

She tried not to laugh. Didn't he realize what he was saying? "You want to be free to go with anybody you want, but I can date only you? That doesn't seem too fair to me."

He was the one who laughed. "Not when you put it that way," he agreed. "But I'm different now, Stacy. Can't we try again?"

She didn't even have to think about it. She shook her head. "It's over," she said simply.

He reached over to touch the ring on her hand. "And you've found someone else?" When she didn't answer, he added, "Maria told me you were going steady with the boy who works at the Bayside."

Maria! Just wait. They were going to have to have a long talk. "Ted did give me this ring," she admitted.

Finally he looked up. "I guess it's too late for me then."

She felt miserable. "Dwayne, I didn't mean to hurt your feelings."

He shook his head. "The guys will never let me hear the end of it. They're already calling you the girl that Miller let get away!"

Stacy couldn't help giggling. She'd been right in the first place. Most of his injuries were to his pride. "Just act mysterious. Don't make explanations. Besides girls love to comfort heart-broken boys."

His expression brightened. "That's true. They really do."

She patted his arm. "You'll be all right, Dwayne."

They went back inside to say good-night to his family. Stacy felt again the force of the family's warmth. Was this what Gran and Aunt Marilyn wanted for her, this united family? Maybe it was that more than success and money. She could almost understand how they felt.

"It's been lovely having you over," Dwayne's mother told her. "Come back again soon."

Stacy smiled, but didn't say anything. Probably she wouldn't be coming back, not with Dwayne.

He let here out in front of her house and she waved good-bye. As she walked slowly up toward the porch, her thoughts were confused. How could she have been so wrapped up in Dwayne a few months ago when now there wasn't a spark of romance left?

"I should be mad at you," a voice said from the shadows on the porch.

"Ted!" She could hear the gladness in her own voice. "What are you doing here?"

"You said you had to work, but when I dropped by the restaurant you weren't there. Your grandmother said she'd given you the night off."

"Gran? This was her night off too. I knew she couldn't stand being away from the restaurant."

"But what about you? Here I thought you were sick or something and came over to check on you, only to find you were out on a date with your former steady." He came down the steps toward her, his face serious. "Look, Stacy, don't make up stories for my benefit. If you don't want to go out with me, just say so. Don't tell me you have to work."

He sounded really angry and for just an instant she was reminded of Dwayne's unreasonable fits of jealousy. But then, she realized, this wasn't unreasonable. He thought she'd lied.

She grabbed his arm so he couldn't move past her. "It wasn't like that, Ted. I did have to work, but Gran overheard Dwayne's mother ask me over for dinner and insisted I go. That's all."

"Oh." He thought about it for a minute. "I'm glad. I didn't like the idea that you'd fibbed to me."

"The worst part is that now I do have to work tomorrow night. Gran really fixed it up good for me."

She would have felt better if he'd looked at least slightly disappointed. Instead he grinned. "Guess we'll just go out on the first night that we're both off duty."

"But if Gran has anything to do with it, that'll be never," she answered glumly.

He frowned. "She really would like to break us up. Funny, usually people don't take such a dislike to me."

"Most people see you in a different setting. They don't think you're a wandering hobo."

"And that's how your grandmother sees me?"

She grimaced. "Only as far as her only granddaughter is concerned. I don't want you to think she's a snob, she isn't."

He folded his arms, looking stern. "Back to the original subject. I've let you lead the talk to other topics long enough. Now I want an explanation!"

"Explanation?" This sudden change of mood left her bewildered. What was he talking about?

"That's right." He leaned authoritatively toward her. "I want to know what you were doing out with another guy when you're going steady with me."

The accusation was unexpectedly painful. It was meant to be a joke, but she didn't think it was funny.

"Come on, Stacy, don't look like that. I was only teasing. You have a right to go out with anyone you choose."

"You too," she choked out the words.

He reached out to cup her chin with one hand, raising her face so that she had to look at him. "What's wrong, love? Bad time with Dwayne tonight?"

She blinked away tears. "Not really. We had a good talk."

"You're not getting back together again?"

"Oh, no, not that. We're just friends."

"That's good. I didn't think he was right for you."

She couldn't help smiling. "You sound like my big brother."

He didn't smile back. His face was very serious. "That's not the way I feel about you, Stacy."

She didn't speak, but held her breath, caught in a moment that seemed too intense for words.

He released her, stepping away. "You're my steady girl," he was joking again and her heart seemed to drop. "And don't you forget it."

She couldn't smile. "I won't," she promised.

The next few days didn't work out as she'd hoped. Ted didn't suggest another date, though he seemed friendly and cheerful every time she ran into him at the restaurant. It was almost as if he'd decided that his invitation had been an intrusion, that the pretense at going steady mustn't be pushed too far.

By Saturday morning, Stacy had about decided that if she ever wanted to go out with Ted again, she'd probably have to ask him.

She was in the kitchen at the Bayside, putting plates in the dishwasher after breakfast and considering that very possibility when Jonas walked in.

"Hi, Stacy. Got some hot coffee left?"

She'd felt different about Jonas ever since his engagement to her aunt was announced. She didn't quite know what to say to him. "Sure," she said. "We always have coffee."

She poured a cup and handed it to him.

"How about keeping me company while I drink it? Things should be kind of slow at this time of the morning."

Stacy glanced over to where Gran was slicing beef for sandwiches. "Sure, honey. Take a break."

Somewhat reluctantly, Stacy followed him out into the nearly deserted dining room.

The big man sat down lightly for all his size, eyeing her warily. "Your aunt is concerned about you, Stacy."

So this wasn't just a casual little chat. Inwardly Stacy sighed impatiently. Gran and Aunt Marilyn wasted way too much time worrying about her. "I don't know why she should be, Jonas. I'm fine."

He sipped his coffee, taking his time about answering. "It's probably a foolish idea, but she seems to think you're opposed to our being married."

"That's dumb. Why would I care?"

He shook his head thoughtfully. "I can see that you might. Your childhood hasn't exactly been the most stable in the world. You don't see a lot of your dad and I don't get the idea you're too fond of your stepmother. Your grandmother and your aunt must mean a lot to you."

"Sure," she shrugged. "But I like Dad, too, and I think Madge is all right. Besides what does that have to do with you and Aunt Marilyn?"

"Maybe you don't want to see any more changes."

She gave that a moment's serious thought. "Come on, Jonas, things are changing all the time. Just when you think everything has settled down and you've got your life planned the way you want, something unexpected happens." She couldn't tell him that she was thinking of Ted. Just when she'd about decided what she wanted to do about Dwayne and going steady, he'd come into her life and changed everything.

"Do you feel that way about my marrying your aunt? That I've messed up all your plans?"

"Don't be silly. I was thinking of something else entirely." She couldn't help frowning a little. "Besides, Jonas, what if I did mind? It wouldn't change things one bit. You'd still marry Aunt Marilyn, wouldn't you?"

He smiled. "You bet!"

She couldn't help smiling back. "That's what I thought. So if you'll just excuse me, I have work to do."

She started to flounce away. "Wait a minute, Stacy."

She turned.

"What I wanted to say was that I've got this cousin over at the hospital in Brownsville. She's a kind of therapist, got a degree in psychology. If you're having trouble handling things, she'd be glad to talk to you and help you work things out. She's really good at that kind of thing. It's her job."

Stacy couldn't help laughing. "I'm working it out, Jonas. I told you I'm fine."

She went to the kitchen and back to work, but she couldn't help thinking about what Jonas had said. Imagine! He thought she needed a psychologist to help work out her problems!

It didn't seem so funny though when she thought of kids like Ted, people who were hurting so badly they didn't know how to go on. Probably there were others like him, lots of them. And maybe they weren't always lucky enough to have friends and family to help them, or maybe the problems were just so serious that they had to have someone with training to help in dealing with them. It must be really special to feel you could help people who were sunk that deeply in their own troubles.

"Did you have a nice chat with Jonas?" Gran asked. She was so darned transparent. Stacy couldn't help giving her a hug. "We talked. Don't worry about it."

"But, dear, you seemed a little upset about Marilyn's marriage."

"I'm working on it. Don't worry," she said again.

"Don't worry about what?" Ted asked from the doorway. "Is something wrong?"

She whirled around. She hadn't known he was anywhere near the place, but there he was, wearing the huge apron Gran had given him. "I didn't know you were working today."

"Sure, I'm scheduled all day."

"Me too."

Gran went back to work, pointedly giving them privacy. Stacy looked at her thoughtfully. Who had slipped up here? She had just come to take it for granted that they'd be scheduled with very little overlapping of time—Aunt Marilyn and Gran saw to it that she and Ted worked different hours.

"This is no way to spend a beautiful Saturday," she said.

"Sure isn't." He grinned, friendly as always, but nothing more.

She couldn't help feeling a little desperate. Had she ruined every chance with him when she'd gone out with Dwayne last Monday to please Gran? "But at least I've got the evening free."

"Me too."

She picked up a damp sponge and began cleaning surfaces as though her life depended on it. They both had the evening off. That had been established. Couldn't he take the lead from there and suggest they do something together?

"What shall I do next?" he asked her grandmother.

She felt like kicking him. How could he be so dense? Couldn't he see she was dying to be asked out?

"You might do some mopping back here while things are

quiet," Gran told him. "Stacy, you'd better take some time off and study for that history test you've been talking about."

Obediently Stacy put down the sponge and went to the little desk in the back of the kitchen where Aunt Marilyn did the accounts. She always brought her books along so that she could study during leisure moments, but right now history was the last thing in the world she wanted to think about.

Gran peeked out front. "Jonas is still out there. I think I'll take him a second cup of coffee and have one myself. I need to get off my feet for a while."

Stacy stared at meaningless words on the pages of her textbook. They marched in blurred confusion before her eyes. She couldn't help being much more conscious of the swish of Ted's mop as he moved about the task her grandmother had assigned him.

Finally she said, "I guess your mother would be really surprised if she could see you now."

"Not too much. She taught me to mop."

"You had to help around the house?"

"Sure. Sean and I always had to help, even more in the last couple of years since Mom went to work. She has someone come in to help with the cleaning, but she says it doesn't do much good if I just make a mess the minute the cleaning person leaves." He grinned.

"What does your mom do?"

"Runs a catering business. She plans big parties, weddings, things like that." He looked thoughtfully down at the wet floor. "She says staying busy has really saved her life since . . . since Dad died."

"She must miss you."

"That's what she says. She wants me to come home soon. Says if I hurry I can still sign up for the summer semester."

Stacy's heart thumped painfully. Chicago was so far away.

She might never see him again. "Is that what you're going to do?"

He shrugged. "I haven't decided, but I promised Mom I'd think about it."

"I'll miss you." She tried to keep her tone light so that he wouldn't guess how terribly much she meant it. "Seems like we've hardly gotten a chance to get acquainted."

"You're a busy girl with school and work and everything. Now in my case, with just this part-time job and what little I do over at the motel, I still have plenty of time to walk along the beaches by myself and think and try to figure things out. I suspect there are going to be lots of years ahead when I think about this time and realize how lucky I was to have it."

She hoped he would remember her when he was thinking about South Texas and the island, but she doubted it. Glumly she turned a page and tried to concentrate on history.

"When I do go back to Chicago, I'm going to feel torn between two places. When I'm here, half the time I'm thinking about Mom and Sean and wondering how they are. But when I'm there, I'll be thinking of you."

Stacy swallowed hard. It sounded as though he really cared about her. She stared unseeing at the pages of her book and heard again the swish, swish of the mop. Was that all he was going to say?

She wasn't going to let it happen this way! Time couldn't just slip away, lost in misunderstandings, leaving her always wondering how he really felt.

"Are you doing anything tonight?" she asked abruptly, not even turning to look at him.

"Nothing special. Why?"

She said it fast before she could lose her courage. "We both have the evening off so I thought we might do something together."

"What would you like to do?" he sounded as matter-of-fact as if it were the most ordinary thing in the world for her to suggest a date. The awful thought struck her that maybe he didn't even see this as a date. To him, this was probably just a suggestion that two friends spend a little time together, kind of like an unexciting evening out with pals.

She turned to face him. "I don't care what we do as long as we're together and have a chance to talk."

"I have this really unique idea," he said, leaning close to whisper as though it were some tremendous secret. "Why don't we go over to the island?"

She smiled. "Something we've never done before!" She couldn't help thinking he might not be so unromantic as she'd thought. The island was the place where they'd met.

"But it'll be different tonight," he told her. "Just wait."

"Different?" she asked, puzzled. What was he talking about?

"I get off at six. How about if I pick you up at about seven?"

She stared in bewilderment at him. "But I get off at six too. Why don't we just go together?"

"Because I have things to take care of first. I'll pick you up at seven. That'll give you time to change. Wear that pretty dress you wore to Mexico. It looked nice on you."

A dress! He wanted her to dress up to go to the island. "OK, if that's what you want," she said unenthusiastically.

Gran came in, flapping her apron in their direction. "We've just had a whole bus full of high school students unload out front," she announced. "You two get out there and start taking orders."

Stacy started toward the dining room, but Ted touched her arm as she passed. "Be prepared for a whole new Ted Lorimer tonight," he warned.

9

It would be summer before long. That was the fact that impressed itself on Stacy's mind as she stepped out on the front porch to wait for Ted. It was spring now, the lush, opulent spring that came with an increased flurry of colorful blooms to this nearly tropical region. Soon Ted would go away forever.

She didn't know why she was surprised that the possibility hurt so much. Smoothing the full skirt of her powder-blue dress, she sat down on the comfortable lawn chair from which Gran liked to view the passing street.

When the old van pulled up, she got to her feet, waiting as Ted opened the door and got out. Her eyes widened. He was more dressed up than she'd ever seen him, wearing dark-brown pants and a jacket in a lighter shade that was close to cream.

"Hi." A little shyly, he lifted one hand in greeting as he approached.

It was as though they'd just met and this were their first date. Stacy's breath caught in her throat. "Hi."

"Ready to go?"

She nodded, picking up her small purse. Suddenly she wished she could run back inside and take one last glance in her mirror to make sure her blonde curls were still in place, her dress unwrinkled, her lips still outlined with coral gloss. But, no! That was just nerves. She'd checked her appearance right before she came out and everything had been fine then. She smiled at him as they walked out to the van. "Gran and Aunt Marilyn are both at the Bayside tonight. They hope to get some planning for the wedding done between busy spells."

"Does that mean you can stay out as late as you like?"

"You know better than that. Gran keeps a strict curfew. If I'm not in on time, she'll probably call the police. And since most of the force eats at the Bayside, they'll be glad to do her the favor of locating her granddaughter."

He grinned. "I'll try to have you back on time then. I don't want to be dragged back by the cops."

Curiosity overcame her as they started across the causeway. "Isn't this a kind of funny way to dress for a picnic on the beach?"

He started straight ahead at the sturdy ribbon of road that led across the bay. "I made reservations for us at the Seahorse."

"The Seahorse?" The name came out in a kind of gasp. She knew it well as one of the most exclusive restaurants on the island, the kind of place where wealthy tourists and locals, dressed in their most elegant clothes, went to dine. She'd never been there. The prices at the Seahorse had been too steep even for Dwayne's generous allowance. She glanced down at the skirt of her simple cotton dress. "I'm not dressed up enough."

"You look wonderful. I asked you to wear that dress because I like the way you look in it."

She glanced nervously out at the bay, hating to bring up the matter of money. He'd said he wanted to be self-supporting while he was here and she knew all too well that he wasn't making a bundle of money working at the Bayside. She hated the thought that he might be blowing a month's earnings on this one evening.

"I'm sure there are lots of other nice places on the island. We don't have to eat at the Seahorse."

"It's first class for us tonight." He grinned. "Though I don't see how the food can be any better than what your grandmother makes at the Bayside."

She smiled uneasily, unable to think of anything else to say without bringing up the subject of money. She thought about offering to pay her share and realized she didn't have more than ten dollars in her purse. That wouldn't go far at the Seahorse!

Night was beginning to settle gently on the evening as they drove onto the gracious grounds of the restaurant, where carefully planted palms and other tropical trees and shrubs waved in a brisk breeze. Feeling a little uncomfortable, she allowed Ted to help her from the van so a uniformed attendant could drive it away for parking. Uneasily she glanced at her companion. Ted seemed like his usual self. Maybe he was used to coming to elegant places like this, but she wasn't! She almost wished they were headed down the beach with a picnic hamper.

"Lorimer," Ted spoke quietly to the head waiter. "Dinner for two."

As they were led through the restaurant, Stacy got an impression of the low buzz of conversation and of crystal, glistening in the soft glow of muted lights. She sank down in the chair the waiter pulled out for her, hoping Ted realized their situation. Surely he must know that eating in a place like this was expensive.

He smiled at her, looking particularly cheerful. "Having a good time?"

She looked around nervously. Everyone in this place seemed to be at least ten years older than they and most looked to be about her grandmother's age. "Oh, sure."

"Liar!" He leaned across to her. "You look like a kitten who suspects a dog is just around the corner."

The description made her straighten her shoulders. She didn't want to look like a kitten; she wanted to look confident and sure of herself, as though she were used to eating in places like this every day of her life.

She lifted the stemmed glass in front of her to take a sip of iced water. The moist base of the glass almost slipped from her hand and she set it down carefully. No point in trying to pretend to a sophistication she didn't possess. "Look, Ted, I've always heard about this place, but I've never been here before. I feel as if everyone's watching me."

He chuckled, leaning closer to whisper. "If I were really smooth, I'd tell you they were watching you because you're so gorgeous."

Her eyebrows raised a cynical quarter of an inch and he laughed. "The truth is, Stacy, that everyone's busy with their own dinner and their own company. They aren't paying any attention to us."

Cautiously she looked around. The couple at the next table were bending toward each other, whispering softly. They certainly weren't paying attention to anyone other than themselves. She looked further. At the table next to the romantic young couple, a cheerful group of what looked like businessmen were in the midst of heated discussion. They weren't noticing her either.

She grinned. "Guess you're right. Nobody's interested in us—at least not until I drop something and it smashes all over the floor."

"You handle dishes practically every day of your life."

She drew a deep breath. "Not in a place like this." She looked down at the menu, then up at him again. "Ted, you can't afford it."

His chuckle was soft, deep in his throat. "I like the way you worry about me, Stacy, but this is special. My big brother is treating us tonight."

"Your brother? But I thought you wanted to be independent."

"I do, but that doesn't mean I can't keep the check Sean sent. It's OK to take a birthday present, isn't it?"

Wide-eyed, she stared at him. "You mean it's your birthday?"

He nodded. "That's right. And this is my celebration."

"But I don't even have a gift for you."

He chuckled again. "How could you? It's the first you've heard about it. Besides, what I wanted most was to spend the evening with you."

Blood seemed to be pumping through her veins at a furious pace, like water pounding on the shore during a storm. "I'm glad you wanted to be with me."

He opened his menu and glanced at her. "Choose something special to eat."

She tried to obey, telling herself it was OK to relax and have a good time now that she knew the evening was not going to be disastrous to his finances. But the lines on the menu were blurred. She looked up at Ted. "Happy birthday," she whispered.

Somewhere in the back of her mind, a sane little voice was telling her that she mustn't care too much. He would be leaving soon and she'd be left to wander the beach where they'd met all by herself. But this wasn't the night for sanity.

"I can't imagine what this birthday would have been like if I hadn't met you, Stacy."

When the waiter approached, they had to ask for more time to study the menu. Stacy finally chose red snapper and Ted ordered prime rib. Then the waiter went away and the world seemed to contract again into the small circle just around them.

He looked different, she thought, from the sad-faced, too-serious boy she'd met on the beach that day. "Have you talked to your mom lately?"

He nodded. "She called this afternoon. Wanted to wish me happy birthday. Said I have to come home before she'll give me her present."

"She must miss you."

"I suppose so. It's been a hard time for her since my dad died, but she's coping. She's strong, I guess you'd say. I keep needing to remember that."

Stacy swallowed. She sometimes forgot what a difficult ordeal Ted was undergoing. She couldn't even imagine how she would manage if Gran or Aunt Marilyn suddenly dropped out of her life forever. "It'll be a long time before it stops hurting, I guess, Ted."

"Probably never. I may forget sometimes, but then there will be moments when it seems just like yesterday that Dad died."

This was no way to be celebrating his birthday, reminding him of his sorrow. "But I'm glad you came here and we met."

He reached across to take her hand, only to be interrupted by the formal-looking waiter who'd come to place salad plates in front of them. Embarrassed, Stacy withdrew her hand and sat stiffly until the waiter departed.

Ted's lips quivered and laughter brightened his eyes. He reached across for her hand and gave it a little squeeze before letting it go again so he could start eating his salad. "I told my mom about you and how much you've helped me get through this. She said she'd like to meet you."

No chance of that. Not with Ted's mom living hundreds of miles from Texas. Stacy was just as glad. Meeting Ted's mom might be a little scary.

"I'd like you to meet Sean too. For a big brother, he isn't bad."

"Next time I visit Chicago, I'll be sure and drop by," she answered with only a light touch of sarcasm.

"Do that."

"I'm glad you dropped by here." She picked up her fork and started to eat her salad. "I don't know what Aunt Marilyn would have done without you."

He started laughing, choked, and took a big gulp of water before answering. "Getting all excited about your aunt's wedding?"

"Oh, sure," she said with total insincerity.

He grinned. "Like that, huh?"

She shrugged. "I don't want to talk about it."

He nodded as though he understood. "Some things are really

hard to say, Stacy. I mean they come out sounding mushy and sentimental, kind of dumb."

Bewildered, she stared at him. One minute, they'd been talking about Aunt Marilyn, and the next, this.

"I don't want to go away without saying how much it's meant knowing you. All by herself, one five-feet-five girl has turned my life around."

"Five-feet-six," she corrected automatically.

"You've made a big difference for me. I can see now why my mom didn't think my coming down here was such a great idea. What I had in mind was wandering along the beaches by myself, trying to figure out the meaning of life."

"I'd think that would have made you feel worse."

He nodded energetically. "I can see now that's exactly what would have happened. You've kept me in the middle of life, Stacy, when I wanted to go the other way."

This time, she was the one to reach across, touching his hand lightly. "I'm glad."

In between bites of salad, he went on. "I'm going back and I'll stick with it this time. I'll enroll in summer school and do my best to make such terrific grades that they won't dare keep me out of medical school."

She tried to smile. This was beginning to sound like the end of something. Was he trying to tell her good-bye?

"It'll be a while before medical school. You've got the rest of your college ahead of you first."

"True. I won't be setting up my medical offices for a while yet. But I did want you to know that I'm back on track. I've wanted to be a doctor ever since I was old enough to think about it, and nothing that has happened changes that."

The waiter came to remove their salad plates, replacing them with the larger plates containing the main portion of the meal. Stacy's fish looked and smelled delicious, but she didn't feel hungry. It was as though she'd swallowed a whole bucket full of beach sand. "You're lucky to have something you really want." She watched him cut his meat.

"It'll come for you too. Lots of people don't figure out what they want until they're in college, Stacy, and you've still got another year of high school."

"I have been thinking about it. After we talked that day at the lighthouse, I thought about what you said—that I'd be good with people. I want to work with people, Ted, not things."

He chewed thoughtfully, looking at her as if waiting to see what else she had to say.

He was right. There was more. "You've made a difference for me, too, Ted. You made me start to think what I wanted to do when I'm grown-up. I'm still not sure, but I think some kind of therapy, something where I can help people get back to a normal life after they've been hurt in some way."

He put his fork down. "Like me? The way you've helped me?"

She laughed a little nervously, afraid he wouldn't take her seriously. After all, her plans sounded terribly vague. "I haven't even looked into it much, but it must be a great feeling to help somebody that way. It could be a person whose trouble is inside her head, or it could be someone who was hurt in an accident and had to learn to walk again or . . . well, or anything. I really don't know yet."

"Some people spend their whole lives looking for the work that's right for them, Stacy, but you've headed straight for it."

She relaxed then, for the first time aware how important it had been that he understand her plans and not make fun of them. "Both of us seem to know what we want."

The bucket of sand had melted inside her stomach and now she was hungry. She picked up her fork and took a bite of the snapper. "This is almost as good as Gran's," she told him.

He grinned. "I wouldn't mention that to her."

After they'd finished the main course, he told her he'd ordered something special for dessert.

"Birthday cake, I hope," she said.

He shook his head. "We're having something else instead."

He wouldn't tell her what they were having and remained mysterious until a waiter approached their table with a small cart. Within seconds, he was preparing a flaming dish and, glancing around, Stacy noticed that the diners at nearby tables were turning in their direction now to watch the preparations under way. She didn't mind, knowing that they were only seeing a young couple having a good time together. When the waiter handed her a dish of dark cherries with ice cream, she smiled at Ted.

"Now that's one thing Gran doesn't make, Cherries Jubilee!

"Better than birthday cake any day."

"But you didn't get to blow out the candles."

"That's OK. I made a wish over a flaming dessert."

"And what did you wish?" Stacy was hardly aware of the waiter's discreet departure.

"Can't tell or it won't come true."

They ate their cherries and ice cream slowly, not talking. The silence didn't bother Stacy, though, because it was a friendly quiet.

After they put their spoons down, Ted grinned at her. "We've got some good colleges in Illinois. My university has the kind of training you'll need."

Stacy stared at him, her mouth suddenly dry. She reached over for her glass and took a sip of water. She couldn't help hoping he was telling her about his college because he wanted her to go there, that he didn't want her to go out of his life forever!

After they left the restaurant, they strolled along the beach together, holding hands. It was getting late when they got into the van and drove back toward the mainland.

"This has been my best birthday ever," Ted said.

"Better even than the ones when you were little and had balloons and games?"

"It's hard to beat those days, but tonight topped them. Even if Sean couldn't be here to make his usual contributions to my party." He glanced across at her with a grin. "Mom always said Sean kept a party lively. When I was three, he put the goldfish in the punch."

"Poor thing! Did it survive?"

"Mom rescued it immediately. Sean seemed to think it had gotten bored swimming in ordinary water."

"What else did he do?" Stacy asked, growing interested. Somehow she'd pictured Ted's brother differently.

"When I was seven, he sneaked half a dozen invitations from the envelope and sent them out himself. Mom had planned a small party with only four or five of my friends, but three of the prettiest girls in the seventh grade showed up too. Sean acted very innocent about the whole thing, but you couldn't fool Mom."

Stacy laughed. "Sounds as if your brother plans his own entertainment."

"You could say that. Dad always said I was the serious one and Sean didn't know how to be serious. It's not really true, of course. When something's wrong, when you need him, Sean's always there."

She couldn't help feeling a twinge of envy at the relationship he described. Her own little brothers were too distant, both in location and age, for them to have this kind of closeness.

"Sean always makes me feel like Gloomy Gus by comparison."

She reached over to touch his arm. "I have lots of fun being with you."

"Then how about driving into Brownsville to that rock concert with me next Saturday night?"

"I wish I could, but Saturday's Aunt Marilyn's wedding. I have to go."

"Oh! So do I. I promised your aunt I'd help with the food."

"I wish that were all I had to do. I have to be maid of honor. Gran said she was too shy to be in the wedding. Imagine Gran claiming to be shy! She just didn't want to have to stand up in front of everyone, so I'm stuck."

They drove back to Port Isabel, where the streets were dark and quiet. He stopped the van in front of Stacy's house. "If we can't make the rock concert, we'll just have to plan on something else."

Stacy felt as though little bubbles of happiness were floating in the air around her. He was taking it for granted that they would be going out again. "I'd like that," she said, knowing it was the understatement of all time.

They got out together and he walked with her up to the front porch where they lingered, holding hands again.

"Stacy," he said softly.

The front door was flung open. "Stacy!" her grandmother said sternly. "It's quite late and time you were in bed." The door slammed.

Stacy's hands trembled in anger. "I'm sorry."

"It must be after midnight. She was probably worried about you." He bent close, touching her lips with his. "Good-night, Stacy."

She went into the house, conscious that he stood out there waiting to make certain she was safe inside. She felt cared for, protected.

Gran was in the kitchen heating milk, a sure sign she was having trouble sleeping. "I did lose my temper, Stacy," she said, an edge to her voice, "but I never expected you to be so late from a picnic on the beach. I was just certain you'd had a car wreck."

Stacy was surprised that all her anger at the unexpected interruption had evaporated. There wasn't room inside her for any such negative feeling tonight. "I hadn't realized it was so late, Gran. But Ted and I didn't picnic. We ate at the Seahorse Restaurant."

"Fancy! I don't see how he can afford such a place on what we pay him. I'm surprised you didn't have to end the evening by washing dishes to pay for your meal."

Stacy didn't want to hear any more of this. "I'm going to bed."

"We don't seem to be as close as we used to be," Gran said unexpectedly, sounding wistful. "We don't mean to disapprove of your friends, but we do want the best for you."

Stacy gave her grandmother a sudden fierce hug. "Ted is the best, Gran." She turned then and fled to her bedroom.

10

Stacy marched slowly down the aisle of the crowded church, wishing that Ted could see her in the long-skirted rose dress that made her look like the heroine of an epic movie. But Ted was back in the kitchen at the Bayside, helping get food ready for the reception.

It had been a busy Saturday: getting her hair done, her dress pressed, making sure the flowers were arranged properly at the restaurant, which had been closed all day in honor of the occasion. She'd hardly been able to say more than a word of two to Ted and now, grumpily, she faced the fact that they were going to be separated for the entire evening.

She looked ahead to where Jonas stood with his best friend, awaiting the entrance of his bride. He looked so dazedly happy that she could almost forgive him for what he was doing to her life.

She took her place at the front and waited as the little flower girl, who was Jonas's small niece, scattered petals along the aisle. Then she felt the tightening attention as the bride appeared. Aunt Marilyn looked absolutely gorgeous in her glittering gown and filmy veil and for a minute Stacy could think of nothing else—not even the fact that fate and her grandmother seemed determined to keep her away from Ted.

She listened to the solemn words of the marriage ceremony, interrupted only once by an exhilarated cry from the smaller of her two brothers. "There's Stacy!" Tommy announced at his sudden discovery of her standing at the front of the assembled congregation.

Stacy's face burned, but she tried to retain her composure. It was nice having Dad, Madge, and the two little boys here for the wedding, but this much public attention was unnecessary. And when the words were all spoken and Jonas kissed his bride, she couldn't seem to smother a growing resentment. Everything was changing. Nothing ever would be the same again.

She drove Gran back toward the Bayside a little ahead of the other guests leaving the church so that they could make certain everything was ready for the reception.

"Wasn't it a lovely wedding?" Gran said, wiping her eyes.

"I don't know why everyone gets so sentimental about things like weddings. People get married every day. It's no big deal."

"Wait until it's your turn. I'll never forget my wedding day, though it was nothing like this. Your grandfather and I just slipped away by ourselves and were married by a justice of the peace. It wasn't an elopement exactly. My parents knew about it, but his didn't. They didn't want us to marry."

"But, Gran! How could anyone possibly disapprove of you?"

Gran laughed. "It *is* possible, Stacy. They thought I was too young and foolish to be a proper wife to their only son. In time, we came to have a very good relationship, but as I started out to say, though we didn't have the flowers and the girls in pretty dresses and the crowd around us, it was still a special day. It's the words, the promises, and feelings, that make it that."

At the restaurant, Stacy went inside thoughtfully. It had been transformed from its everyday appearance by the flowers Gran had mentioned. A long table with a lacy, white tablecloth featured a huge, cut-glass punch bowl and a multitiered wedding cake.

"Everything look all right?" She jumped at the unexpected voice interrupting her thoughts.

She turned gladly to Ted. Before she could speak, he whistled softly. "Hey, you look great!"

"Thanks." Uncomfortably, she smoothed the full skirts of the dress. She didn't feel like herself in it. "Things look good here too."

"I'm afraid I can't take credit for that. The crew your aunt hired has done most of the work."

Gran came in. "Hi, Ted." She headed right back to the kitchen to check on things there.

"Guess everyone will be arriving any minute so I'd better get back to work."

Stacy nodded glumly, feeling close to tears for no reason that she could imagine. "You're lucky you don't have to stay out here and pretend to be having a good time."

He stepped toward her with quick concern. "What's wrong?"

She closed her eyes tightly to squeeze back the tears. She would not cry. "I don't know. I just feel rotten."

"About the wedding? Don't you like Jonas?"

"It's not that. He's one of my favorite people."

"Then what is it?"

She turned away from him to stare at the wedding cake. "It's not something I've figured out, but I just feel kind of down for no reason I know. I must be a truly terrible person to be upset because my aunt is so happy."

She felt his hand on her shoulder. He turned her around so that she had to face him. "It's Ted, Stacy. You don't have to pretend to feel any different from what you really feel."

It was hard to meet his eyes. "But I don't even understand it myself. I want Aunt Marilyn to be happy and I like Jonas, but I guess I'm a little afraid I'll be left out." She tried to laugh and failed. "Doesn't that sound selfish?"

"It sounds honest. Lying to yourself is always a mistake, Stacy."

"Oh, Ted, what do I do?"

He soothed the side of her face with gentle fingers. "You tell yourself it isn't so awful to feel the way you do—that even though you were small when your mom died and your dad left, it's still made a difference. And now things are changing with the people who brought you up and you're scared a little."

She closed her eyes. "I guess that's it."

"But, Stacy, if you'll look through my eyes, I'll tell you what I see. I see an aunt and grandmother who are so crazy about you that nothing can change it. And I see that the guy your aunt is marrying has been fond of you since you were a little girl. You should hear the way he talks when you're not around. People would think you were his own kid."

Stacy's lashes lifted. "Really?"

He nodded. "If you give Jonas a chance, I think he'll fit right into your family."

He used the tail of his long chef's apron to dry her eyes. She felt comforted as much by his concern as by what he'd said to her. "Thanks, Ted."

He grinned. "No extra charge."

She was still smiling when the guests began to come in and he had to rush off to the kitchen. She found herself lost in a swirl of greetings and congratulations as half the town seemed to move along the reception line and then to the tables heaped with food. She'd been too busy greeting everyone else to get anything to eat herself and she looked up with surprised gratitude when a tall man handed a heaped plate to her. "Thanks, Dad."

He nodded. "Let's find a place in the corner where we can talk and eat. We've hardly had a second to ourselves."

It was like Dad to make sure they had a little time to themselves on the rare occasions they were together. The found two
chairs a little away from the others and sat down.

"I'm starved." Stacy put a fork full of shrimp salad into her
mouth.

"Good food. Just what you'd expect at the Bayside."

"Gran did do some of the cooking, but Jonas insisted most
things be catered. He said Gran and Aunt Marilyn should have
some time off."

Dad nodded. "Jonas will take good care of Marilyn."

The remark bothered Stacy a little. "And she'll take care of
him. That's the way it works, Dad."

He grinned, his thin face seeming to broaden. "My little girl
is growing up."

"I should hope so. I'll be 17 in September."

"And you'll be coming up to spend the summer with us as
usual? This new boy in your life isn't going to change that?"

So Gran had been talking. "Ted will have gone home by
then. He's only here for a little while." Each word she spoke was
a facing of the painful truth. It was hard even to imagine the
summer without Ted.

"I always count on those summers. They mean a lot to me."

She looked at him with surprise. "I would have thought they
were a real hassle, trying to fit me in with Madge and the boys.
We don't always get along too well."

"But still you're my daughter and you mean a great deal to
me." This was a lot from Dad, Stacy knew. He had a hard time
talking about his feelings.

"Anyway, Stacy, I wanted you to know that I realize I haven't
done much for you these years you've been growing up. But I
have been planning for your future. I don't make a whole lot of
money, but back when you were born, your mom and I started a
little savings account for you. We wanted you to have some of
the educational opportunities we missed."

Stacy stared in shock at her father. This picture of a young couple making plans for the faraway future of a tiny baby was so unexpected. Dad always had seemed too wrapped up in his small sons and his second wife.

"Mother says that she and Marilyn have paid you for working here over the years and that you've saved most of that. With what I've put away, you should be able to go to just about any college you want, within reason."

Stacy couldn't help thinking about what Ted had said. Maybe they'd be able to go to college together!

"Thanks, Dad," she mumbled, hardly knowing what to say.

"It makes us feel good to be able to do it," he told her, sounding more like himself again. "It was your mother's idea in the first place. She talked about it even before you were born. As for me, I never had any idea that putting away just a little regularly could mount up so over a long period of time. Madge and I have started saving for the boys' educations now."

Stacy wondered if he were as uncomfortable as she was. They'd never had much to say to each other, but it did give her a warm feeling to know he had given this much thought to her welfare.

She was a little relieved to see Gran approaching. "You two are looking so serious," she accused.

"We were just talking about Stacy's future," he explained.

Gran grimaced. "I don't even like to think about the fact that she'll be going away to college in only a little over a year."

Her son shifted position awkwardly. "You've done a great job with her, Mom."

Gran beamed proudly at Stacy. "I think so."

Stacy tried to smile, feeling acutely uncomfortable. Why did occasions like this always bring out the sentiment in people? It was embarrassing.

Dad seemed to feel the same way. He got to his feet. "Guess I'd better go help Madge corral the boys. They're a handful these days."

Gran watched him leave before departing. "They're spoiling

my grandsons," she said. "Two rowdier little boys I've never seen."

"Suppose you could do better?" Stacy grinned and Gran laughed.

"That Ted is working his head off back in the kitchen." She skipped to another subject without warning. "He's been a real mainstay in getting ready for this wedding."

A compliment for Ted? One of Stacy's eyebrows slipped upward a little. What was going on here? "Somehow I got the idea you weren't too crazy about Ted."

"I guess I have been a little rough on him, but he's a hard worker. Does a good job too."

"And he is good-looking."

"I don't see what that has to do with anything, Stacy."

Stacy looked over to where Aunt Marilyn and Jonas—Uncle Jonas—were chatting in a circle of friends. "They look so happy."

"They are," Gran said with quiet conviction. She looked questioningly at Stacy. "But I've had the feeling you weren't too pleased about the match."

"I was scared and a little jealous, I guess." Stacy looked down at the empty plate she still held in her lap. "Ted talked to me about it. He helped me see that I've got to give Jonas a chance."

"Ted did that?"

Stacy nodded. "He's been through some troubles of his own, Gran. He sees a lot more deeply than most boys his age."

"Well!" Gran sounded impressed in spite of herself. "About this going-steady business . . ."

Stacy wondered if she were going to bring up Dwayne again.

"I guess you're old enough and sensible enough to make up your own mind."

She got up then and went back over to supervise the cutting of the wedding cake. Stacy stared after her in shock. This was turning out to be a very surprising day.

Moving quietly through the crowd, greeting friends as she went, she headed in the direction of the kitchen. Ted was busily working alongside the people brought in just for the wedding. "Hi," she called. "How's it going?"

Grinning, he came over to her side. "Let's just say I don't plan to make a career of kitchen work."

"You must be doing a good job because you managed to impress Gran, which isn't easy." She reached down to slip the onyx ring from her finger. "You can take this back now, Ted. Gran is finally convinced that I'm mature enough to choose my own dates."

He seemed a little reluctant about taking it. "It was fun while it lasted."

"For me too."

He held up the ring so that it glistened in the light. "This doesn't mean we can't go out together any more, does it?"

"I don't see why it should."

"Then how about if we go see a late movie after I get off work tonight?"

"I'd like that. And, Ted, even if you aren't my steady, I'd like you to go to the spring dance at school with me, if you don't mind going to a high school dance?" The invitation was out before she thought it through. It was the big event of this semester at school and most of her friends had accepted dates weeks ago. But everyone had assumed Stacy was going with her "steady."

"When is it?"

"Just a little over three weeks from now, on a Saturday."

"Sure, Stacy, I'd love to go."

She went back into the wedding crowd, knowing she must be wearing a cloud of happiness around her. Ted was going to the dance with her. She could hardly wait.

The weeks before the dance passed quickly because she and

Ted dated regularly. On the big evening, she put on her new dress, a long, peach-colored gown with narrow shoulder straps and a fitted bodice. It made her feel glamorous.

When Ted came by for her, he brought a corsage of white carnations, which she pinned at her waist. As they went out to his van, he grinned at her. "You don't even resemble that girl who found me on the beach. Are you sure you're the same one?"

Stacy laughed happily. "I certainly am."

The night was soft, humid, and the sky was filled with stars. Stacy went inside the gym where the dance was being held, feeling triumphant. She was proud to show Ted off to her friends.

Maria was one of the first people they met. "I was beginning to wonder when you two were going to show up."

Stacy glanced apologetically at Ted. "I told her we were coming."

"That doesn't surprise me." He started looking around. "Where's Rob?"

"Who?" Maria's face wrinkled into a puzzled frown.

"Rob Cooper, the boy who went to Mexico with us."

"Oh, he's over there." Maria pointed to where Rob was dancing with a pretty girl in a white dress.

Stacy giggled. "Rob is two boyfriends back for Maria. You have to keep in touch or you lose track of what's going on in her social life."

He frowned at her with mock ferocity. "I hope you're not like that, Stacy?"

"I don't see what's wrong with it," Maria complained. "It's going to be a long time before I'm ready to settle down to just one boyfriend."

"Nothing wrong with it," Ted assured her. "But for some strange reason, that's not what I want for Stacy."

Maria frowned again. "You told me this going-steady thing was only for show."

Ted looked quizzically at Stacy. "I thought you told her everything."

"Just about everything." She stuck out her bare hand. "Look, no ring. We're not pretending to go steady any more."

Maria's dark eyes widened. "But that means you're not here because of your grandmother or the pretending."

Ted nodded. "It means we're here together because Stacy asked me and I wanted to come."

Maria stared at them for a moment as though trying to figure out if they were playing some kind of joke on her. Finally she nodded. "Come on, meet Carlo."

"Who's Carlo?" Ted asked.

Stacy slipped her hand into his. "He's the latest love of her life, of course."

Ted met Carlo and half a dozen other couples who were friends of Stacy's and Maria's. She was pleased to see how well he fit in with her friends, but she couldn't help noticing that he was obviously a little more mature than her high school friends. That made her remember that he was older, that he would be going home soon to go back to college.

They'd danced to a couple of lively numbers played by the band that had been hired for the occasion and were drifting happily in each other's arms to a slow dance tune when she happened to look up, startled to see an unexpected face only a couple of feet away. Dwayne!

He was behind Ted, dancing with a popular girl who was almost as pretty as Maria and who always had her choice of boyfriends. She was surprised that she didn't even feel a twinge of jealousy at the sight. Dwayne was welcome to date every pretty girl in high school and college if he'd just stay out of her life. At least, she didn't have to be afraid he would disturb her evening with Ted.

"What's wrong?" Ted drew her a little closer.

She couldn't believe he was so perceptive. No need to tell

him she'd been upset by the sight of Dwayne. "Just thinking how thirsty I am. When this dance is over, we'll have to get some punch."

He nodded, looking puzzled, but when the music ended, he guided her toward the punch table. She was able to breathe a little more easily, somehow instinctively wary of an encounter between the two boys, though she couldn't have said why.

Certainly Dwayne had been bad enough about making scenes over nothing when they were going together. But the last time they'd met, he'd been more than reasonable and now he had a girl friend and no reason to be jealous.

Ted had handed her a cup of punch when Maria came running up, Carlo just behind her. "Stacy, Dwayne's here!"

Stacy glanced uneasily at Ted. "I know," she admitted. "I saw him."

Ted took on a look of annoyance. "So what's the big deal? It's been ages since you went steady with him."

"You don't know Dwayne," Maria informed him. "I remember one time when he had an absolute fit just because Stacy was talking with another boy at a party."

Stacy was embarrassed. "It was at the end, right before I broke off with him. He didn't act like that at first."

She didn't like to have Ted think that she'd let Dwayne push her around. It hadn't been like that, but for just a little while she'd been confused. Everyone but Maria had been telling her how lucky she was to have Dwayne and it had taken time for her to figure out that she didn't agree with them.

"Don't worry, Stacy, I won't let him bother you."

She smiled at him. She couldn't tell him that the only thing she was afraid of tonight was that Dwayne would cause him embarrassment.

"Dwayne was really nice the last time I saw him. I'm sure he's forgotten all about me by now and we're worrying about nothing."

The words were hardly out of her mouth when Sabrina, the pretty girl she'd seen dancing with Dwayne, strolled up. She didn't look exactly happy to see them. "Hi, Stacy, Maria, Carlo. This must be your new boyfriend, Stacy, the snowbird from the north." The way she described Ted came out as an insult because of the tone she used.

She turned away, not even planning to introduce them, when Dwayne came up, looking for his date. He reached for Sabrina's arm, but dropped it abruptly when he saw Stacy.

"Hi, Dwayne," she said.

"Hello." His gaze went on to take in her date and his face darkened angrily. "Hello, Lorimer."

Ted nodded, barely courteous.

It was hard for Stacy to understand what was going on. When she'd seen Dwayne that night of the dinner at his home, he'd been polite, even a little friendly. But now, because Ted was here, he was different.

She put her full cup of punch back down on the table and tucked her hand under Ted's arm. "This is my favorite song. Let's dance."

Ted looked at her as though he guessed that she didn't even know what was playing. "Drink your punch first, Stacy," he said quietly.

She glanced at Dwayne's set, angry face and picked up her cup again. She sipped the punch, suddenly needing its moisture in her dry mouth. Nobody said anything and even the bubbly Maria seemed to be waiting for what would happen next.

Sabrina grabbed at Dwayne's hand. "Come on! Let's dance." He ignored her. "I thought you'd be gone by now, Lorimer."

"I'm still here."

"I can see that. Thought Stacy had better taste."

Stacy stood her ground uneasily. It was with relief that she saw the principal heading across the crowded dance floor toward them.

11

Mr. Jergins walked right past them. Stacy watched him go by a little wistfully. If only the principal had come over and said something, acted just slightly official, then maybe the tension that seemed to circle them would have gone away.

But nothing was changed. Dwayne was still glaring at Ted and Ted was still standing there with that same patient look.

"I don't like the idea of Stacy's running around with someone like you, Lorimer. Think I'll just talk to her grandmother about you."

"Gran knows all about Ted and she likes him," Stacy told him indignantly.

This defense only seemed to make Dwayne more angry. He took a step toward Ted.

"I came here to dance," Sabrina declared. "And I guess I can find someone who'll pay attention to me." She flounced furiously away. Stacy really couldn't blame her.

She put her cup down again. "I want to dance," she echoed, more firmly this time. Finally Ted looked down at her and smiled, seeming like himself again.

Suddenly Dwayne lunged at him, throwing a short punch that landed on his right eye. Ted grabbed him by both arms, managing to restrain the other boy so that Dwayne danced frustratedly, unable to land a second punch.

Stacy heard a girl cry out, sensed the attention of the dancers turning toward them. "Dwayne!" she yelled. "Stop that."

"He's stopped," Ted said grimly, keeping his firm grip on the other boy.

"Now, now! What's going on here?" The principal frowned as he headed back in their direction.

Stacy couldn't help being annoyed. Wasn't this just the way things worked out? Where was Mr. Jergins when they needed him?

He pointed angrily at Ted. "Release that young man," he demanded.

Obediently Ted let go of Dwayne, who looked at him as though he'd like to launch another attack. "Dwayne," Stacy reprimanded softly. He stepped back sullenly.

Mr. Jergins was looking at Ted, not Dwayne. "We expect our students to behave during occasions like this."

"I'm not a student here," Ted replied with courteous formality, nodding in Stacy's direction. "I'm a guest of Miss Whitman."

Stacy couldn't help feeling a little glow of pride at how grown-up he sounded and looked. Compared to him, Dwayne was acting like an angry little boy. "That's right, Mr. Jergins, and Dwayne started the whole thing."

The principal ignored her. "I don't believe we've met before," he told Ted.

"I'm visiting the valley. My name is Ted Lorimer."

"Well, Ted, I'm afraid I'll have to ask you to leave the dance. We don't need troublemakers coming in to cause problems among our own youngsters."

"But, Mr. Jergins!" Stacy exclaimed. "It wasn't Ted's fault."

"No, it really wasn't," Dwayne spoke in a sulky voice. "I guess I just lost my temper."

Mr. Jergins smiled indulgently. "If that isn't just like you, Dwayne, to try to cover for someone else." He frowned at Ted. "I don't want to have to ask you to leave a second time."

Ted's face was an angry red, but he didn't betray his feelings in any other way. He looked questioningly at Stacy. She stepped over to take his hand. "Let's go."

"Us, too," Maria insisted. "We don't want to hang around with a crowd like this. Come on, Carlo."

Stacy caught one last glance of Dwayne's face as they left. He looked totally miserable. At least he'd ruined the dance for himself as well as for them.

Carlo's car followed the van to the Bayside, but Maria rushed ahead of the others into the little restaurant. "Just wait until you hear what happened, Mrs. Whitman!" she yelled.

The four of them told Gran what had happened, words spilling out so that she had to hold up a hand to stop them. "Wait a minute! I'm not getting this clear. Did you say Mr. Jergins hit Ted?"

Ted was the calmest of the four. "You talk, Ted," Maria instructed.

Quietly and without undue drama, he explained what had happened. "I guess it's natural enough for him to believe the boy he knows rather than the one he doesn't," he finally concluded the story.

Gran folded her arms across her chest. "That Dwayne," she said. "I'm shocked."

"He has an awful temper, Gran. He does things like this and then he's sorry. He tried to get Mr. Jergins to listen to us."

Gran shook her head. "I'm glad you listened to my advice and quit going steady with that boy."

"Listened to your advice!" Stacy started to explode, then saw the twinkle in her grandmother's eyes. "Oh, me, too," she added meekly.

Gran turned to Ted. "As far as Harry Jergins' listening to

Dwayne because he knows him, fiddlesticks! It's because his father's on the school board and he's afraid he'll make a fuss if he throws his son out of the dance. In the first place, that's an insult to Dwayne's dad, who is the fairest man in the world; in the second, he might as well learn that just because you're from out of town doesn't mean you don't have someone to stand up for you."

She whirled around to march back into the kitchen. They could hear her giving instructions to her assistants; then she came back out, pulling off her apron as she headed toward the door. "Come on."

"Where are we going?" Stacy asked, running after her.

"I'm going to have a little talk with a certain principal."

"You can't do that, Gran."

"I don't see why not," Maria said. "Go get him, Mrs. Whitman."

Ted was grinning as he headed the van back toward the gym. Gran had a determined look on her face, and Stacy could turn around and see Carlo's little sports car following close behind. Maria wasn't going to miss a thing!

But Stacy had a feeling she was about to be humiliated publicly. Mostly Gran was cheerful and easygoing, but when she got her temper up there was no stopping her. No telling what was going to happen now.

Gran was the first one out of the van at the brightly lighted gym and the rest of them trailed after her as she headed inside. When the teacher who was acting as the ticket taker tried to stop her, she put him in his place with one look of determination. "I need to see Mr. Jergins."

"Go right on in, Mrs. Whitman. I'm sure he'll be glad to see you."

"Don't be too certain of that, young man," Gran told the teacher, who was nearly her own age. She sailed past him and out into the crowded dance area.

"It's all right, Gran," Stacy whispered. "You don't have to say anything."

"We do not sit quietly and allow injustice." Gran spotted her quarry and headed across the floor.

Stacy looked up at Ted. What must he think of the goings on tonight? He grinned and squeezed her hand. "Come on. Let's give your grandmother our support."

"Yes, let's hurry," Maria urged from her other side. "I don't want to miss anything."

Even though she would have preferred to retreat, Stacy had little choice but to advance, moving carefully through the clusters of high school students. Gran was beginning to attract a certain amount of attention as the students noticed her progress through the crowd.

Poor Mr. Jergins was standing on the sidelines, energetically lecturing an apparently wayward student. He didn't even see Gran coming.

Stacy, who was trying to hang back but was being virtually pushed forward by her friends, couldn't help hearing Gran's first words. "Good evening, Harry," she said as though it were a polite social call.

He turned around and the student he'd been lecturing made a quick escape. "Oh, hello, Dovie." He frowned. "What are you doing here?" He looked past her to where Stacy and Ted stood and his frown deepened. "You shouldn't let Stacy bring some troublemaking outsider here to one of our dances," he reproached her.

A delicate pink flush darkened the area just over Gran's cheekbones. "You will have to admit, Harry, that I've always been supportive of your actions at school. If you've said Stacy was a problem, I've always corrected her."

"But Stacy's never actually been a problem."

"Putting that entirely aside, Harry, if Stacy had been a problem, I'm sure you know I would have backed you up. I'd have seen that she behaved."

Stacy felt Maria's elbow, nudging her own. A small crowd of students was forming around the two adults.

"I'm sure you would have, Dovie," Mr. Jergins admitted.

Gran was small, not quite five feet tall, and plump so that she looked like a jovial Mrs. Santa Claus most of the time. But right now she was dignified enough to make up for what she lacked in inches. "That's why I'm sure you'll listen to me now when I want to register a complaint."

"Well, of course, Dovie." He took out a handkerchief to wipe his perspiring brow. "We'll go somewhere private."

"That won't do," Gran interrupted. "The boy was insulted in public. He has a right to be defended in public."

"Well, let's not make a mountain out of a molehill, Dovie. It was just a little disagreement between the boys, and you know boys will be boys. . . ."

Gran turned around to indicate Ted's face with one dramatic gesture. "A little disagreement gave our Ted here a black eye?"

The area around Ted's eye was faintly purple. "We don't have to make a big deal of this, Mrs. Whitman," he said, looking a little uncomfortable now that everyone's attention was on him.

"Yes, we do. What we have here is a nice young man who comes on a visit, brings my granddaughter to a dance at her high school, and is thrown out for no fault of his own. That's not right, Harry."

Mr. Jergins tried to stand his ground. "I was informed that he started the fight."

"Who told you that? Did Stacy say Ted caused the fight, or that he struck a single blow to Dwayne?"

"Well, I can't remember exactly."

"You didn't listen to my granddaughter! In fact, you had a good number of young people here who must have witnessed the whole thing, but you didn't wait to hear what they had to tell you."

"It was my fault." A voice sounded from behind Stacy. "I tried to explain that."

She turned around to find a very depressed-looking Dwayne standing behind them.

Gran looked sympathetically at him. "I can understand a boy's losing his temper and I certainly admire his willingness to admit he was in the wrong." She glared fiercely at Ted. "You two shake hands."

Stacy had to hide a grin behind one hand as the two boys shook hands as instructed, neither of them looking particularly happy about it.

"If that's all cleared up, we can go on with the dance," Mr. Jergins said, sounding more like himself as he waved the students back out on to the floor. "I hope you're happy, Dovie." He turned to Gran.

She patted his arm. "I know it's a big job keeping all these young people in line, Harry."

He grinned at her, looking almost boyish in spite of his advanced years. "We could use another chaperone, Dovie. You could stay and help me see that things are kept in order and maybe you and I could even dance a little."

Stacy's mouth was still open as Ted led her away. "That's some grandmother you have," he whispered as they moved out onto the floor to the soft strains of a popular ballad.

Stacy chortled happily. "I'll probably never live it down. I can just imagine what the kids are going to say. But can you believe it? After all the things she's said about you, she really stood up for you."

"It was great. It's something I'll always remember when I think of the time I spent here."

Stacy looked up at him with sudden alarm. He almost made

the time they'd spent together sound as if it were already in the past tense. She moved a little closer to him. "You talk as though you're going away tomorrow."

"Not that soon. But it won't be long. When I talked to Mom this morning, she said Sean was flying out to meet me. He wants to spend a couple of weeks, kind of a little vacation, and then we'll go home together."

Two weeks! Panic struck her. He was going away and she'd never see him again. "How soon is your brother coming?"

"I'm supposed to meet his plane in Brownsville Tuesday evening."

She could hardly think of what to say. It seemed so final and Illinois was so far away. If only she knew for sure she'd be seeing him again! "You're going to summer school then?"

He nodded. "That's why I've got to get back to make the arrangements. It'll help me make up for some of the time I missed."

He sounded so cool, so matter-of-fact. Maybe it didn't mean as much to him as it did to her. She missed a step, came close to stumbling, and he steadied her. "I can't wait for you to meet Sean. I just know you're going to like each other."

She managed a stiff, frozen smile. "I'm sure we will."

The rest of the dance was sheer misery. Even the sight of Gran, looking shorter than ever in the arms of the tall, thin Mr. Jergins, did little to raise her spirits. And when Gran invited a group of Stacy's closest friends back to the restaurant for a private party after the dance, she had to pretend to be pleased. Everyone else seemed to have a terrific time and it was close to two o'clock when the party finally broke up.

All Stacy could think about as she watched her friends leave was that soon Ted, too, would be going away. Miserably, she wished that the days would inch by—she didn't want them to hurry past because she had such a little time left with Ted.

They helped Gran clean up, all three of them yawning sleepily. Afterward Ted saw Gran safely to her station wagon and then he and Stacy went out to his van.

"It was fun tonight," he said, seeming lost in thought.

Stacy yawned again as he started to follow Gran from the Bayside's parking lot. "Which part did you like best, getting punched by Dwayne or being marched back in there to face Mr. Jergins?" she asked.

He laughed. "You've got to admit we had some good moments in between. I always have a good time when I'm with you, Stacy."

It was only a few blocks from the restaurant to home. Gran was just getting out when they pulled up.

Ted leaned out the window to thank Gran for the party. All three of them knew he was really thanking her for more than that, for standing up for him to the principal. Gran smiled. "You're all right, Ted. Best cleanup person I ever hired."

Ted grinned. "That's a compliment I never thought I'd get. But, Mrs. Whitman, you're going to need a new employee. I've got to go home in about two and a half weeks."

Gran looked shocked. "Go home?"

He nodded. "I'm going back to college and I need to go to summer school to make up for missing this semester."

She seemed to be torn between being pleased and being disapproving. "I told Marilyn you were a boy with plans for the future, but you just weren't saying much." She looked uneasily at Stacy, as though aware of the pain this parting would cause her. She looked back at Ted. "We want the best for you, Ted." she said quietly. "Guess I'd better get inside. A woman my age needs her beauty sleep. You'd better put an ice pack on that eye, Ted."

She went inside and Stacy moved closer to Ted. She nodded agreement with her grandmother. "You really are developing a black eye. You'd better get right home and put ice on it the way Gran said."

"In a minute." He reached out to grasp one of her hands, pulling her even closer. "I've got something to say first."

Uneasily, she looked up into his eyes. "What's that?"

"That I'm going to miss you," his voice was hoarse, "that I've never known anyone in my life like you before."

Confused and tired, she hardly knew what to say. "I'll miss you too, Ted."

He reached into his pocket and pulled something out. "How about making if for real, Stacy?"

She had to bend closer to see what he was holding out to her. It was the onyx ring, gleaming in the moonlight that streamed in the wide windows of the van. She shook her head. "I don't understand."

His voice was husky, close to a whisper. "I want us to go steady again, only for real this time."

Stacy stared at the ring, then she looked up into his face, trying to take in what he was saying. It was hard to go in one minute from depression because he was going away, to this great surprise, that he was asking her to go steady.

But that didn't change anything. He was still going away.

"You're leaving. In a little more than two weeks, you'll be going home."

"But that's why. I love you, Stacy, and I can't just go away as though . . . well, as though, it's just all over."

He bent toward her and their lips touched. Stacy was too tired and mixed up to think clearly. For a minute, the only thought moving through her brain was, "He loves me."

They pulled apart. "I have to get inside. Gran will be waiting up for me."

He held the ring out to her. "You haven't put this on your finger yet."

She stared down at it, wondering why she was hesitating. Ted was very special. She'd never felt this way about anyone before. And yet she wasn't sure she wanted to put his ring back on.

"I'll be coming back out to spend some time before the fall semester starts and then next year we can plan on going to college together. Won't that be great?"

Stacy tried to smile. "Sure. Great."

He reached out to touch her hair with one gentle finger. "What is it, Stacy? What's wrong?"

A smile trembled on her lips. She did love him. Why then this hesitation? Maybe she was only tired. "I went steady once before and it turned into something awful. You saw how Dwayne acted tonight."

"I'm not Dwayne."

"I know that, but. . . ."

"Stacy, you're so worn out you can't even think. Go inside now and get a good night's sleep and we'll talk again in the morning. You can give me your answer then."

She didn't even protest as he ushered her up to the front door and gave her a quick kiss. She felt something pressed into her hand. "That's the ring," he whispered. "I hope to see you wearing it when I pick you up tomorrow. I'll let you sleep late. See you at about ten-thirty."

She nodded. "Put some ice on that eye." She went inside to find Gran, already dressed in gown and robe, waiting on the sofa for her. "Gran?" she whispered softly.

Gran had fallen asleep. She sat up abruptly at Stacy's call. "What? What?"

Stacy leaned over to give her a kiss. "Just wanted you to know I'd come in. Good-night."

She went on to her room and changed into her pajamas, but before she turned out the light she stood examining the onyx ring. Thoughts chased each other through her head: how she'd felt going steady with Dwayne and how it had been like getting out of prison when she finally gave his ring back. But Ted was different. She was older now and she really cared about him.

If she said no and he went away, she'd probably never see him again. The ring would be something to tie him to her, to bring him back at the end of the summer. Her mind was made up. She had to say yes. She had to go steady with him.

In the morning, she would slip the ring on her finger and go out to meet him, waving it in the air so that he'd know immediately what her answer was. She couldn't help smiling at the thought of how he'd look when he realized.

She put the ring down on top of her chest of drawers, turned off the light, and crawled into bed. Tomorrow she would tell Ted the answer was yes. She would go steady with him.

12

She slept soundly, without dreams, and when Gran's voice awakened her, it seemed as if it were still the middle of the night. "Phone call for you, Stacy."

"Be right there." She still felt as though she were climbing out of the deep waters of sleep. Reaching for her robe, she wound it around her as she headed out to the kitchen and the phone. Aunt Marilyn was sitting at the table, having a cup of coffee with Gran.

Stacy nodded at them both and picked up the receiver. "Hello."

"It's Dwayne, Stacy." The masculine voice on the other end of the line sounded unaccustomedly humble.

"Dwayne," her own tone sharpened. "What do you want?"

"Just to say I'm sorry I made an idiot of myself. It won't happen again because I've learned my lesson."

"I should hope so."

"Look, Stace, my only excuse is that you really matter to me. It hurts when I see you with someone else."

"But, Dwayne, we're not going steady any more." Stacy lowered her voice, glancing at Gran and Aunt Marilyn, who were trying to hide their interest. "I gave you your ring back ages ago."

"But that doesn't mean we can't be friends any more, does it?"

"I guess not, but . . . ."

"And that we can't go out together once in a while."

"I don't think that would work."

"You may be right, but I want you to know that I still feel special about you, Stacy."

Uncomfortably she managed to say good-bye and hang up. He'd used almost the same words to her that Ted had, but she didn't like to compare the two situations. Ted and Dwayne were very different.

"It was thoughtful of him to call and apologize," Gran said.

"He'll be a fine young man when he grows up a little." Aunt Marilyn agreed.

Oh, no! They were pushing Dwayne at her again.

"Ted is a fine young man too," Gran said quickly. Aunt Marilyn nodded vigorously.

Gran got to her feet. "I've got to do a few errands this morning. Marilyn, I'll leave you with Stacy to entertain you."

Stacy looked thoughtfully at her aunt. She waited until she heard the door close behind her grandmother. "Gran's being subtle. What did you want to talk to me about?"

Aunt Marilyn grinned. She looked particularly happy these days, Stacy thought. "She's worried. She's afraid you're letting yourself care too much about Ted."

"So what's wrong with that?" Even though she didn't usually drink coffee, Stacy poured herself a cup and plopped down in a chair. She still felt half-asleep.

Aunt Marilyn took a minute to answer, studying Stacy with kind eyes. "You're just asking to get hurt, hon, falling for a guy who's going to be hundreds of miles away."

"So she told you about that too?"

"She mentioned it. Neither of us wants you to sit around, dreaming about some guy from another state while your friends

are out having fun. Play it safe, Stacy, don't . . ." Abruptly Aunt
Marilyn stopped, a funny look on her face. Then she laughed.
"Listen to me. Here I am giving you advice on how to lead your
life when I put off getting married for years because I was afraid
to make a commitment."

"You were scared to marry Jonas?"

She laughed again. "It wasn't Jonas. It was marriage. Being
responsible for another person and, oh, everything else. But,
Stacy, it's not so bad. Having work you love and a person who
loves you, that's just about the best life has to offer."

Stacy grinned. "I've been thinking about the future and I've
about decided to go to college next year. I may become a physi-
cal therapist."

Aunt Marilyn looked a little startled. "I didn't know you'd
made such definite plans."

"Not definite exactly." Stacy looked down at the table. Nothing seemed very definite right now, just confused.

Aunt Marilyn got up and went to rinse her coffee cup in the
sink. "I've got to go. The Bayside may not open until evening
on Sundays, but my husband likes me to be home for lunch.
He's making it."

She said this with such pride that Stacy couldn't help smiling
again. "Thanks for the advice, Aunt Marilyn."

Aunt Marilyn wrinkled her cute little nose. "I didn't exactly
come to any wonderful conclusions for you, did I?" Suddenly
she looked serious. "If it really matters, Stacy, don't let it slip
away. If it matters, it'll stand the test of time."

The house seemed quiet after her aunt had left. Stacy wan-
dered aimlessly through it, trying to figure out what she'd meant
about time. Everything was so mixed up. She went into her
bedroom to stare again at the onyx ring.

Going steady with Dwayne had been a nightmare, but Ted
was different. She was older now and her feelings for him were
more than those of a girl simply impressed by a boy everyone

else thought was wonderful. She'd like Ted even when her closest relatives disapproved of him.

But still, what would it be like to go steady with a boy who was only a voice on the telephone, a letter in the mail, and an occasional visit? And what would it be like for him?

She couldn't help remember her final thought from the night before. The reason she'd finally decided to go steady with him had been fear. If she let him go back without having put his ring back on her finger, then she was risking everything. He might fall for someone else.

Stacy was startled when she glanced at the clock and realized it was already after ten. Ted would be here within minutes! She rushed to take a shower and dress and was still brushing her hair when the doorbell rang.

Glancing down at the ring still on the vanity in front of her, she hesitated. She started to put it on, then stopped. She couldn't do it. Fear—the wish to tie a boy to her—was not a good reason to go steady. Besides, it couldn't be done. Even an onyx ring didn't provide any guarantees.

Slowly she went to answer the door. His face was expectant as he looked eagerly at her. Stacy swallowed hard, concentrating her attention on his injured eye. The area around it was a technicolor blend of purple and deep blue, with subtle shadings of pale green. It was swollen half-shut.

"I see you didn't get the ice on quickly enough."

He shrugged as though to say a little thing like a black eye couldn't bother him today. He looked down at her hand.

She put it behind her. "Ted," she said, "come on in the living room. I want to talk to you."

He didn't move, but his expression hardened. "It's no, isn't it?"

He reached for her arm, tugging gently until he forced her hand into his own. He looked at her, waiting for her explanation of the ringless finger.

"I care a lot about you," she whispered, "but I'm not sure yet. I don't think I'm ready to go steady."

He stood, motionless as a mountain. "I see."

"I hope you understand."

"Oh, sure, I understand." His tone was cold, bitter. "These last few months just meant more to me than they did to you."

"No, Ted, that's not true."

He didn't look at her, wouldn't meet her eyes. "If you'll just give me the ring back, I'll leave."

She wanted to argue, wanted to talk until that stiff look left his face so he would be her Ted again, but she didn't know what to say. She went into the house and returned with the ring.

He took it and started down the walk away from her.

She couldn't let him go like this. "Ted!"

He didn't turn. "What?"

"Nothing."

She didn't really believe that he would just go away without giving her a chance to explain until she heard the engine of the van start. Her heart seemed to sink to her toes as she watched him drive away.

When Gran came home, she found Stacy still sitting on the steps of the porch, too numb even to cry. Maybe she'd only gotten what she deserved. She'd been selfish, unwilling to give up her freedom to go to parties and to go out with other boys, uncertain about her own feelings and how grown-up they were. And now Ted was gone. Sensitive and easily hurt, he would never forgive her. She was sure of that.

She saw him the next day at work, but only for fleeting moments because he seemed to be avoiding her. When they did meet, he looked so forbidding that she didn't know what to say, but felt a dull ache all over as though she might be coming down with the flu. The next day, she did manage to aim a smile in his direction. "You must be excited about your brother's coming in today."

"Sean has been delayed. He won't be here until tomorrow." He went on with his work and she dashed back to the kitchen in a rage, swearing not to make another attempt at being friendly.

It was Aunt Marilyn's day in the kitchen. "What's going on?" She glanced up briefly from the huge bowl of salad she was preparing.

"Boys!"

"That's a fairly inclusive group."

"First it was Dwayne and now it's Ted. They don't even seem to think about my feelings."

Aunt Marilyn turned her full interest on Stacy. "Ted seems to be more perceptive than that. What's wrong? The two of you have a fight?"

"He asked me to go steady. I told him I didn't think it would be a good idea since he's going away." Unhappily, she stirred the thickening broth for the day's homemade soup. "I like Ted a whole lot, Aunt Marilyn. But I can't help feeling that it would be wrong for us to go steady. I'd rather be with him than anyone, but when he's not here I just can't stay home all the time. It wouldn't be right for him either."

Aunt Marilyn nodded. "Pretty smart of you to see that."

"But he doesn't understand at all. He's just angry."

"Did you explain it to him the way you just did to me?"

"I tried to. He wouldn't listen."

"I see." Aunt Marilyn added shredded carrot to the salad. "I suppose you'll forget about him as soon as he's back home again."

"No! It's not like that. I'll never forget Ted. But I'm not ready yet to make commitments, not even as much as I'd like to tie Ted to me. Dwayne was practically the first boy I ever went with and look how that worked out. I've got to find out who I am before I'm ready to go steady or be engaged or anything like that."

"Engaged! You're only 16, Stacy. I do hope that's a few years away yet."

Stacy smiled. "Sure it is, though I do have a couple of friends who want to marry as soon as they get out of high school. But I have other plans, and so does Ted. That's what you meant, isn't it, when you talked about time? If we're right for each other, it'll still be there when we're older."

Aunt Marilyn nodded while she seemed to be thinking hard.

"The trouble is the distance. If he goes away angry, then we may not get a second chance. I'll probably never hear from him again."

Aunt Marilyn poked thoughtfully at the salad. "Did I forget to tell you, Stacy, that Jonas and I will be picking you up after school tomorrow? We're looking at a house and we'd like to see what you think of it."

"A house? To buy?"

"Sure, why not? Can you go with us?"

Stacy nodded, trying not to feel hurt because Aunt Marilyn had dismissed her own problems so easily. It was exciting to be looking at new homes. She couldn't really be blamed if she had trouble focusing on Stacy's love life. A little sadly, she thought that it was only one of the changes to be expected now that Jonas was part of their lives.

The next day after school, she waited impatiently, wondering if Aunt Marilyn had forgotten her request. She was about to give up and walk home when a familiar old van drove down the street and stopped in front of the school.

Ted got out and walked toward her, smiling cautiously as though not sure of his welcome.

Stacy still didn't understand. "I'm supposed to meet Aunt Marilyn and Jonas."

"I came instead."

Her heart beat faster. "Don't tell me Aunt Marilyn's done it to me again!"

"She thought you might like to drive to the airport with me to meet my brother. She said it would give us a chance to talk."

The fluttering feeling in her chest seemed to be spreading to her brain. She couldn't think. "I thought you didn't want to talk to me."

He opened the door of the van and she climbed in. He went around and got in on the driver's side. "We've got to get going right now or we won't get to Brownsville in time to meet Sean's plane."

"Maybe you'd better just drop me by the house."

"If that's what you want, but I'd like you to go with me."

It was all she needed. "OK"

He grinned as he started the van. "You're hard to convince."

"I'm not the one who was angry."

He nodded, not saying anything as he drove out of town. "Your aunt had a few things to say and she forced me to listen. She made a lot of sense."

Stacy stared out at the passing palms. They had a chance again now, thanks to Aunt Marilyn, but she was almost afraid to speak. It would be too easy to blow this opportunity and the idea that he would go away angry made her feel sick. "I guess Aunt Marilyn and Gran will never learn not to interfere in my life."

"This time I didn't mind. They were on my side."

Stacy leaned back, trying to calm her racing brain. They would need every mile of the distance to Brownsville if they were to have a hope of working this out. "What did Aunt Marilyn say after she got you cornered?"

"She said you liked me in spite of the fact that I was a thick-headed dolt."

That sounded so like her aunt that Stacy couldn't help laughing. "It's true," she confessed softly.

"She tried to tell me how you felt about going steady and how it wasn't time yet. She seemed to know that we weren't really going steady before."

"That's funny. I didn't tell her."

"She must have guessed."

Precious minutes slipped by before either of them spoke again. Panic stirred Stacy's thoughts as she tried to come up with just the right thing to say. At least five miles passed before Ted finally glanced at her again. "Was what your aunt said right? It was just that you didn't feel ready to go steady again?"

"I tried to tell you that."

He stared straight ahead. "I know you did. It's just that it scares me, going away when we've had so little time to get to know each other. It's as though everything could melt away. I want to hang on to you."

"I don't want to lose you either," she whispered. "I will go steady, if that's what you want."

He didn't say anything for a long time, but kept looking straight ahead, his face a stony mask that she couldn't read. They were on the outskirts of Brownsville before he spoke again. "There's a little box under the seat on your side. Pull it out."

Obediently she reached under the seat, located the box, and took it out.

They were approaching the little airport. He waited until he'd found a parking space and brought the van to a halt before turning to her, concentrating all the attention of his serious gray eyes on her. "Open it."

She opened the box. The onyx ring lay inside. So this was his answer. She looked up to meet his eyes.

"I'd like you to wear it, if it won't bother you too much. Maybe it'll help you to remember me until I come back at the end of the summer."

A plane zoomed overhead, coming in for a landing, "That could be Sean's flight," he said. "We'd better get going."

She stretched her left hand toward him, extending the ring with her right. "Put it on for me, please."

"It's what you want, Stacy, not going steady, but just a ring."

"I don't need a ring to remember you by," her voice was unsteady, "but I want to wear it anyway."

With trembling fingers, he slipped it on, then gave her a quick kiss. "Maybe by the time I come back you'll be ready to go steady."

"I'm just glad you are coming back."

"And next year, we'll try to go to school together. I guess I've been a little selfish, trying to talk you into my school. We might meet halfway somewhere."

She laughed. "We have lots of time to talk about that. Come on, we're going to miss your brother."

They ran together across the parking lot toward the terminal. Holding hands, they raced to the spot where passengers were just disembarking.

Ted waved at a tall man who looked like a slightly older version of himself. "There's Sean!"

She smiled up at him and he circled her shoulders with one arm, drawing her close against his side so that they stood together, waiting for his brother to reach them. Stacy blinked back tears as she watched Sean hurry toward them. In another couple of weeks, she would be waving good-bye to Ted. But he would be coming back. Feeling the warmth of his arm around her, she was suddenly very sure of that. He would be back.